**Bl...**

A shout of congratulations erupted from his teammates
as the warhead slapped wickedly into the plane's rear,
tearing it completely free and spilling a massed ball
of living and half-living bodies onto the dirt below.
Suddenly it was a contest between the two light machine guns as to who would reap the greater harvest.
Each gunner sent long streams of red tracer into the
stuggling mass of flesh and bone. . . .

# BORDER MASSACRE
by Greg Walker

# BORDER MASSACRE
## GREG WALKER

JOVE BOOKS, NEW YORK

BORDER MASSACRE

A Jove Book / published by arrangement with
the author

PRINTING HISTORY
Jove edition / October 1990

All rights reserved.
Copyright © 1990 by Greg Walker.
This book may not be reproduced in whole
or in part, by mimeograph or any other means,
without permission. For information address:
The Berkley Publishing Group,
200 Madison Avenue, New York, New York 10016.

ISBN: 0-515-10423-X

Jove Books are published by The Berkley Publishing Group,
200 Madison Avenue, New York, New York 10016.
The name ''Jove'' and the ''J'' logo
are trademarks belonging to Jove Publications, Inc.

PRINTED IN THE UNITED STATES OF AMERICA

10  9  8  7  6  5  4  3  2  1

## DEDICATION

For all the "55," who served with honor
but no recognition.

There's a CIB owed every swinging Richard who
stepped into the breach from La Union to La
Libertad. Someday someone with enough balls is
going to right that wrong. In the meantime, we
can only remember our forgotten war in the
privacy of our secret hearts.

# CHAPTER

## 1

The desert is quiet except for the sounds of men and animals as they clamber up the narrow rock-strewn trail leading from the ravine's floor to the plateau's top. Overhead the sky's face is strewn with thousands of blue-green stars, whose brilliance is outdone only by a full moon. Man and animal are huffing in the thin air of the high plains, both burdened by the weight of what they are carrying. For the burros it is a 250-pound load of cocaine per animal, each burden worth millions on the streets of America. In the hands and strapped across the backs of the men it is armament: assault rifles and submachine guns meant to provide protection against either the narcs who are the drug runners' mortal enemies, or the human jackals of their own kind who seek to plunder the nightly convoys coming across the border like half-mad lemmings headed for the sea.

Caza Casanova shrugged mightily in the saddle as his

horse gingerly picked its way up the narrow trail. The M2 carbine he carried was balanced across the well-worn leather, just behind the horn, Casanova's right hand loosely gripping the weapon's wooden pistol grip. He'd folded the parachutist stock shut, knowing that should something happen he'd be forced to fire from horseback, using one hand while the other attempted to control the animal he was riding. Caza liked the M2 for just that reason. It was light, compact, carried a 30-round magazine, possessed a fully automatic capability, and if you knew the weapon you could do a lot of damage in very little time. Around his middle the heavyset gunslinger wore a thick leather belt with a high-ride holster on one side, a long, sleek sheath knife on the other. Caza preferred automatics to wheel guns and had recently picked up a hot Glock 10mm from a gringo college student who was financing his way through school as a free-lance burglar. The knife was Mexican, made by Casanova's uncle years before. It was a good knife, well worn and expertly used by the man who now carried it.

Casanova was himself pure Mexican. He had just celebrated his forty-second birthday and was currently making his fifty-fourth trip across the border. Caza was a professional smuggler, an experienced hand at moving dope, people, guns, and sometimes even money across the invisible line separating New Mexico from Mexico. A combat veteran with the 25th Infantry in Vietnam, the home boy from Los Angeles had drifted after leaving the army, working both in Mexico and Central America until discovering that moving dope into the United States was both profitable and exciting. He'd begun his career as a "foot soldier" for some powerful local authorities with ties to the cartel in Mexico City. A former NCO, Casanova took charge naturally, ensuring each trip across the border was a success with no losses incurred. Drawing on his connections in Los Angeles he began learning how the Border Patrol and DEA operated, often reading manuals "liberated" from their offices by low-paid cleaning personnel out to make an extra buck. Soon he'd moved up, commanding impressive burro trains worth millions and hiring the best gunmen he could find in Houston, San Diego, and Phoenix. The unique thing about Caza Casanova was that his name could not be found in any of the crime computers so heavily relied upon by U.S. law enforcement. He was an unknown factor in the high stakes game of international drug running, an integral cog that was necessary to make delivery, sometimes at the cost of men's lives.

A light, cool breeze skated down the deep ravine's corridor, causing Casanova to tug the felt green beret he'd taken from the body of a reservist down lower over his ear. They'd stumbled across the team several months ago, the man left to stand watch asleep next to the tiny fire around which the rest of the men were wrapped up in their down sleeping bags. The army often sent members of its reserve forces into Arizona and New Mexico, giving them missions to watch certain stretches of the border for night travelers like Caza and his band of merry men. Apparently the team found snoozing didn't think much of the potential threat they faced, left alone under the desert's sky, as their weapons were neatly stacked and unloaded to boot.

Casanova had always carried a major grudge against the Green Berets. In Vietnam he and his buddies had watched the motherfuckers strutting around the bases in their fancy camouflage uniforms, high-speed CAR-15s and hard-to-get 9mm pistols always within hand's reach. They treated the line doggies like shit even though companies like Casanova's lived to make contact with the gooks, the 25th's "Wolfhounds" a respected threat to the NVA and VC in their Tactical Operational Area of Responsibility (TAOR). It hadn't bothered the cold-hearted Mexican a whit to borrow from one of his men a Super 90 riot gun, its extended tube maxed out with 00 buck, and calmly blow each of the sleeping men away in a rapid barrage of gunfire that took only nine seconds to execute. They'd stripped the bodies of anything valuable and undamaged, Caza rewarding himself with the detachment commander's beret, its triple-lightning bolt cloth flash bearing a set of silver captain's bars along with a bright smear of drying blood.

It had taken only a few hours to bury the bodies and erase any sign of the overnight camp's presence, then Casanova's band had moved on to link up with their counterparts over the border.

The burros were moving well their heavy loads seemingly unimportant as they trudged up toward the top of the ravine where the sky opened up in all it's splendor. The pack train had made good time since leaving the load-out point over in Mexico. They'd been on the trail for three days now, following a winding course laid out by Casanova, one which took advantage of the terrain's natural arroyos and canyons to both hide and shelter them. At times they could hear the gringos in their Apache attack helicopters scouting the miles of barren desert for any trace of a cross-border intrusion, the hearty sound of the rotors reminding each man of how dangerous his chosen profession was. It was a known fact the Americans could, and would, open fire on identified drug convoys such as theirs. Several had been lost already, their progress tracked and reported by small teams of what Casanova believed were professional military recon personnel. Of course the American public never read about these attacks in the press, not that the drug warlords could voice a complaint to either Congress or the United Nations.

Caza was positioned in the middle of the train so he could watch their backtrail as well as what was taking place up front. He'd sent a three-man horse party ahead to scout the plateau, their orders to report back as soon as they'd cleared at least three hundred meters of ground from the lip of the canyon's walls. With fifteen burros and nearly thirty men involved, the chance of being ambushed was slim although not nonexistent. Casanova and his bosses were more concerned with rip-off artists than with the DEA and Border Patrol, knowing there existed within the dope world a subculture of renegades and highwaymen that earned its living raping targets of opportunity presented during the movement and transfer of major shipments like the one being escorted. That was why Caza demanded the amount of weaponry his teams carried, and it was also why he possessed the most talented craftsmen in the trade as soldiers.

Tapping his horse's flanks with the heels of his boots, the trail boss eased by a panting pack animal and began moving up toward the head of the column. He could tell everyone was awake, the chance of walking blindly off the trail and dropping into the ravine's guts present in everyone's mind. Even so it had been a quiet trip, with the occasional rattlesnake presenting the only danger anyone had been confronted by since leaving Mexico. Still, Casanova felt suddenly uneasy. It was the quiet which surrounded them that seemed strange, a quiet not of the desert itself. The Mexican had sensed this same unease before, in Vietnam, usually right before everything went to shit. Urging the animal onward, he tapped a rider

gently on the shoulder as he squeezed past, looking upward and nodding so that the man understood his *jefe*
was concerned. Caza heard the low *click* of a rifle safety
being released, the man grasping the situation immediately and preparing for the worst before it happened.

I hope the hell they don't hit us down here, Casanova
thought to himself as he passed a second outrider, alerting
the man with a nudge of the M2's barrel. We can't get
turned around and we can't get over the top if they do,
he mused. Glancing around him he noted they were
bunched up fairly close, each burro not more than five
feet behind the one in front of it. It'd be a shooting
gallery, he thought cursing inwardly. We've got to pick
up the pace before—

From atop the ravine on the opposite wall a series of
powerful miniature stage lights exploded into life. The
drone of several portable Honda generators fractured the
desert's natural symphony, their power fueling broad
beams of high intensity light now pinning the mule train
like hostile butterflies under their glare. "What the
fuck . . . !" growled Casanova as he swung the carbine's
barrel upward so the weapon's forestock lay across the
upper portion of his left elbow, now supporting it should
the Mexican need a steady platform for a shot. A murmur
of alarm began racing the length of the caravan, safeties
clearly audible as weapons were armed, several of the
men slipping from their saddles and hoisting their weapons over them, using the horses as cover from the unseen
enemy's megawatt eyes.

The voices reached Caza's ears even as he was beginning to take up the slack in his trigger. For a moment
it was a totally alien sound, terribly out of place and
definitely from another time in Casanova's violent life.
Then he understood what it was he was listening to, and

the realization left him stunned senseless. Vietnamese! The language was Vietnamese and with its lilting sing-song intonations a flood of grim images burst through Caza's buried memory bank, twisting his face into a mask of both hatred and fear. Seconds later the night was torn asunder as a nearly perfectly executed volley of rifle fire knocked all fifteen mules off their feet, dropping them stone-cold dead in their tracks. It was impressive shooting, especially at night, thought Casanova as he unleashed a half a magazine just above and to the right of the center spotlight. Somewhere along the line the fucking dinks must have learned how to shoot!

Pushing off from the saddle, the former infantryman felt the solid impact of several high-caliber rounds as they thudded into his mount's side. As the animal reared up in pain, another round slammed through its thick skull, splashing Casanova with brain matter as he dived over the still hump of a burro's cooling carcass. All along the steep trail his men were attempting to return fire, seeking to blow out the lights that were pinpointing them for the phantom gunners atop the ridge. Caza recognized the steady hammer of an M60 light machine gun as it joined in the fray, a second death guitar getting in tune from the Viets' opposite flank. Casanova buried himself behind the burro's fleshy barrier as huge chunks of shale and dirt began showering down around him, the machine guns strafing the hapless *pistoleros* without mercy.

Suddenly a cry went up to the right and above Caza's improvised bullet catcher. He recognized the depth of the scream as soon as the tortured voice reached his ears. Some poor bastard had just been put to the knife! A burst of high-pitched, angry Spanish erupted over the battle as one of Casanova's men went hand-to-hand with an infiltrator coming in from the trail head. Bastards! They were pinning his people down and sending in sappers armed with knives, hatchets, machetes, and God knew what else to finish the job! Casanova stole a look down the trail and watched in horror as a knot of his own men collided with a fast-moving team of Vietnamese head-hunters. Knives flashed in the surreal light of the lamps' illumination; blood spurted into the dark as arteries were severed; cries were choked off as fingers turned into talons and tore deeply into unprotected flesh. The LMGs were silent now, with only the occasional rifle shot an-nouncing that a target had been sighted and eliminated amidst the gory *mano y mano* taking place between the two enemy forces.

Casanova took stock of his position immediately. He knew he was being hit by someone as outside the law as he himself was. Old Man Canales would lose some big investment money over this, he thought. Not to mention the millions the coca would have been turned into once on the streets. This was one of the biggest shipments of the year, an attempt by the cartels to replenish what they'd lost in L.A. the year before. Nine other trains had been launched across the border this last week, each carrying over three thousand pounds of coke and heroin to destinations in California, New Mexico, and Arizona. Although most of the coke had come from the fields of Colombia and Bolivia, the heroin had found its way through Burma and across the ocean to where it had been broken down and packaged along the Baja coast. Now Casanova was losing his portion of the shotgunlike dump-ing of dope down the Yankees' throats, and to a bunch of gooks at that!

Caza knew he'd be lucky as hell to punch his way out of this one. The Viets were using standard tactics, tactics he'd seen a hundred-and-one times before. The heavy guns were well dug in and possessed interlocking fields of fire. His men would never touch them with only light weaponry. It seemed obvious that they were outnumbered at least three to one, standard odds in favor of the offensive team. The use of the lights had been brilliant, their effect both surprising and blinding the drug smugglers as well as their transports. Casanova couldn't go forward, as that would mean a hundred-foot fall at best. The wall behind him offered no sympathy, and his flanks were rapidly being eaten up by the oncoming Viet raiders. His only hope was to sucker someone into him, and then fight his way through one of the blocked flanks, probably heading downhill.

Slipping a fresh magazine into the M2 and chambering a round, Caza slipped the loop from over his knife's handle, sliding it free from its handmade sheath. Dropping his head over against the slain beast's belly the Mexican opened his eyes wide, feigning death as the first of the Viet assassins spotted his position in the remaining spotlight's glow. Casanova watched the man scamper toward him, a long-handled tomahawk held low. The killer's companions were finishing off two of Caza's *compañeros*, unaware of their comrade's attention to Casanova's apparently dead body.

When the Viet was close enough to see the strong sparkle of life in Caza's eyes, it was too late. Casanova swung his double-edged blade upward and in, catching the startled thug well below his belly button, where the eight-inch blade sunk to nearly its broad hilt. Feeling the blade cease its forward motion, the Mexican rolled forward onto one knee, ripping the knife across the man's gut until he felt the blade bump up against a hard set of ribs. Because of the double-edged format of Casanova's blade, he didn't have to waste time removing the knife for a second cut. Instead, the veteran blademaster simply spun on his knee, drawing the knife back through its original cut and across virgin territory until it reached the opposing rib wall.

He never ceased to be amazed at the volume of vital organs and intestines that were packed into a man. Pulling the knife back Caza barely avoided the flood of guts that poured out of the Viet's quickly emptying lower torso. The man was screaming to high heaven, his eyes rolled so far back into his skull that the orbs showed pure white. Pushing the living dissection away from him, Casanova ducked as a second Viet swung a machete across his front, the blade slicing thin air.

All thought was gone now. The Mexican didn't hear himself bellowing like an enraged bull, his curses intermingling with those of his assailants as he thrust, spun, parried, and suffered stinging cuts and grazes from their weapons. Caza knew he couldn't allow himself to be pushed up against the wall and pinned. He wasn't planning on a last stand, like those jerks at the Alamo did a hundred years before. No, Caza Casanova wanted to live, and he understood his only chance was to fight harder, meaner, and better than those facing him.

A third Viet reared out of the semidarkness, in his hands a short-barreled shotgun. Caza drew the Glock and in a single motion triggered three 10mm ball busters downrange, striking the trooper squarely in the chest. A hand grabbed the Mexican by his hair, the force jerking his head rearward so that the throat was exposed. Spinning the knife so its point faced backward, Casanova rammed the blade home. He felt the hand loosen just as a sharp edge cascaded off his throat and cut into his shoulder. Twisting the blade sideways, Caza tore it free, running several more steps down the trail before dropping to one knee to send another five rounds from the Glock back the way he'd come.

It was guts-ball now, no holds barred and no quarter given. From across the ravine came a burst of Vietnamese, no doubt from the hit team's commander, thought Caza as he dropped the first magazine from its well. Below him he could hear other voices, falling back it seemed. Dropping to his belly he targeted the first of three spotlights that were still lit, blowing their frames out with two rounds apiece so that the lower trail was once again plunged into bittersweet darkness.

Now he had a chance.

Hugging the ground like a demented lover, Casanova began scrabbling down the broken trail, feeling bits of rock and flesh squeezing between his fingers as he moved. A massive burst from one of the 60s carved a long, jagged break in the ravine's wall directly along Caza's route of travel, showering the desperate man with loose dirt and shale fragments. Along the way he was forced to crawl over, and sometimes around, the bodies of his once-living companions. We never had a chance, he moaned inwardly, the obvious betrayal of their plans evident in the perfect execution of the ambush. Suddenly he was up and running, obeying mental commands directed by his deeply ingrained desire to survive. For some reason unknown to Casanova there was no sound of gunfire chasing after him, a fact that only became important as he watched the powerfully built Vietnamese rise up from out of the trail like a devil conjured up by the Prince of Darkness.

Caza rode the Glock out of its holster in one swift motion, only to feel it torn away as the Viet delivered a fierce snap kick that caught the highly dependable piece

of tactical Tupperware squarely alongside the slide. The
man attempted to follow the surprise move with a rear
kick using the same leg, only to grunt in disappointment
as Casanova ducked under the ripping blow, whipping
his still-bloody combat knife once again from its sheath.
The message was clear: kill the Viet in hand-to-hand and
go free, or accept the fact that he was going to die in
this blasted wasteland.

Several flashlights popped on from up the trail, where
the victors now were gathered to watch the two com-
batants. Caza could clearly see his attacker now, and the
long, curved *khukuri* the Viet had balanced atop his right
shoulder, its wicked cutting edge gleaming in the soft
light provided. Casanova knew about *khukuris*, having
seen several carried in Vietnam by his own men, as well
as a few Down South in Guatemala and El Salvador. A
frightful implement, the *khukuri* was capable of lopping
off a man's hand at the wrist, a lower leg below the knee,
and even a head. Despite his own large battle blade's
advantage against lesser knives, Caza realized he was
outgunned by the man now attempting to draw him in.

The Viet leaped forward, his free hand whipping out
like a lance at Casanova's face as he attempted to distract
the Mexican's attention away from the already moving
*khukuri*. Caza slipped sideways, slashing away from his
direction of movement so that his own knife caught the
Viet's left wrist as it passed by his head, cutting it deeply.
The man barked as the sting of the successful counter-
move raced up his arm's web of nerves, his brain reg-
istering the failure of his assault at the same instant as
the pain of Casanova's blow hit its circuits. Spinning on
his forward foot, the Viet followed Caza's attempt to
circle around him, and the *khukuri* snapped forward at
Casanova's head as if the Viet wanted to cave it in with

a single powerful blow. At the last minute, as Caza pulled his skull rearward, away from the oncoming strike, the *khukuri* dropped and bit deeply into the Mexican's upper foot, splitting it as if it were a hard-shelled crab.

Casanova twisted away from the Viet, whose labored breathing was only drowned out by the cheers of his comrades as they sensed the fight coming to an end. Hopping now, terrified to put any weight whatsoever on the destroyed member, Caza swung the knife wildly at the *khukuri*-wielding Oriental. His uncoordinated movements destroyed whatever sense of balance he still possessed, and even as his mouth opened in a hideous scream of protest the damaged foot slammed onto the ground in a vain attempt to keep Casanova upright. The Viet charged forward as an unearthly bolt of sheer agony blew Caza's eyes, mouth, and hands open. His treasured bowie flung into the darkness, its clattering heard by all as the heirloom bounced off unseen rocks into the ravine's cryptlike maw. Casanova's mind caught the whirl of the *khukuri* as individual snippets of frozen time, each frame bringing the horrible blade closer and closer to its target. He felt the forward portion of the blade burying itself in the side of his neck, the awesome velocity generated by the Viet as he leaned into the kill driving the blade-heavy edge deep into Casanova's upper chest cavity. Then it was dark, a warm rush of steamy blood washing Caza's life away even as the knife was wrenched free from his splintered sternum.

Caza's body was left where it had fallen, the victor removing a Rolex GMT from its dead owner's hairy wrist before the Viet trotted up the trail to join his already busy friends. Men were stripping the heavy loads of cocaine from the dead mules' pack trays, dumping them onto sturdy canvas stretchers, then hurrying these up to the trail head, where each was neatly stacked in piles four loads high. The bodies of the smugglers were being attended to by a second crew, each picked up and swung well out into the void of the ravine's depth. Fallen weapons were quickly inspected for damage, the ones deemed worthless tossed in after the corpses. Atop the ridge opposite the trail stood a small knot of men, their conversation muted as they oversaw the clean-up operation.

Within thirty minutes it was over. In the distance they could hear the powerful whine of the choppers as they raced less than twenty-five feet above the desert's floor toward the now-lit LZ prepared by the raiding parties' pathfinders. The newly acquired cargo would be hastily loaded aboard the surplus Hueys, then flown to a safehouse, where it would be broken down into more manageable packages. These would be moved overland by various means of transportation to distribution sites scattered throughout the country. The victors of the evening's bloody foray would remount their ATVs and head east, arriving back on the highway within hours. From there they would be shuttled back to the city in semitrailers especially outfitted for this purpose.

As the first of the slicks came to a graceful hover above the sandy touchdown point, a tall, lean Vietnamese gave a wave of his hand to the men below him. General Duc Phong was supremely pleased with his commandos' performance, even though he'd lost several more men than he'd considered during their pre-mission planning. Ordering one of his bodyguards to call in the general's personal chopper, Phong calmly lit a cigarette, drawing deeply on the paper tube. He had made much money tonight, millions if the final tally equaled his accountant's computations. He'd also made some major enemies by ripping off the Canales people's shipment. Enemies who would bear watching as they thrashed around seeking the source of their loss.

In the weird glow of the battle's aftermath, Phong watched as Casanova's body flew gracelessly out over the ravine's pit, swallowed by the waiting darkness as gravity welcomed it to the rocks below. The Mexican had fought well, almost to the point of earning himself a shot at surviving the desert's challenges, had he but vanquished Sergeant Quan's *khukuri*.

"*Sin loi, señor,*" whispered the retired ground forces commander, whose division had once been the cream of the South Vietnamese Army. Sorry about that. A gentle tug at his elbow told the general it was time for him to quit the field of battle, and with a flick of his wrist he said his last good-byes as the still-burning cigarette carved a blood-red gouge out of the night's blackness, falling as it did into the already fermenting mass grave below.

# CHAPTER

# 2

Beaumont "Bo" Thornton stepped back, taking the brief moment allowed him to adjust the *tenutui* where it had slipped from its perch on his head. A cushion between his scalp and the traditional Japanese *men*, or helmet, its position had shifted slightly when Tanaka-san's bamboo sword found an opening in Thornton's desperate defense. The ensuing connection between sword and helmet had dropped the retired master sergeant to his knees, a gong-like tolling inside his skull telling him he should have zigged instead of zagged.

From the edge of the practice mat Jason Silver struggled to keep a smile from escaping. Similarly attired in the traditional kendo outfit as worn by Thornton, Silver would be next to face Tanaka. Both men had taken a week off from their daily routine to fly down to Los Angeles, where Rod Tanaka maintained his dojo. An eight-degree Dan, Tanaka was considered to be one of the few kendo instructors who taught sword combatives as it had been done in Old Japan. His fees were high, with Thornton and Silver paying nearly $2,500 apiece for their week's worth of private instruction. Both shadow warriors considered the money well spent, given their outside work for the government as SPRING-BLADE operatives. Jason held his own *shinei*, or practice sword, so that it lay across his padded upper thighs, the bamboo shaft's finish dented and creased by reminders of previous "lessons" like the one Bo had just been taught.

"What are you smiling at you low-life scum-suckin' dog-breath?" Thornton finished putting his helmet back in order; his head wouldn't be so easy.

Tanaka, standing several steps back from his bruised student, launched a stern look toward Silver. Of pure Japanese stock, the man looked awesome in his sparring equipment, every bit the ancient samurai whose art he taught only to those willing to submit themselves to his tutelage. Silver couldn't keep his Adam's apple from bobbing in his throat as he caught Tanaka-san's invitation to step onto the mat, knowing he was in for some serious individual hands-on attention for his simple transgression.

"He's gonna kick your skinny ass, boy. Don't watch his eyes! That was my mistake. He trick-fucks you by looking like he's gonna smack you in the chest, when he's really going for someplace entirely different. Bastard's got it down to a science, as you might have noticed." Thornton limped off the mat, his right knee still sore from yesterday's series of instructions on how to take a man down using the sword to dismember the leg below the knee. The fact that Silver seemed fit as a fiddle annoyed the former One-Zero, whose body appeared to be collecting welts and bruises far more than his companion's.

Silver went on to survive nearly twenty minutes on the mat before Tanaka signaled they were finished for the afternoon. All three men bowed to each other, then began discussing the day's activities as they headed for the kendo master's private shower room. Tanaka treated his exceptional clients well, knowing they were paying an extravagant fee for his time and knowledge. These two were of special interest to the American samurai, their reaction times and killing instinct much more advanced than many of the hobbyists he taught. For Tanaka they were a refreshing change of pace.

After a fifteen-minute sauna, rubdown, and steaming hot shower, the trio moved to Tanaka's spacious office, where Bo made a call out to Phill Hartsfield at his Garden Grove shop. Hartsfield, a highly respected custom blade maker, was the man who'd crafted Calvin Bailey's deadly sword cane. The weapon had drawn blood in San Francisco when he and Thornton had been set upon by a band of gay blades while SPRINGBLADE was pulling Ricardo Montalvo's ass out of a particularly hot fire. Thornton wanted a Hartsfield *katana* for himself, while Silver was looking for a *khukuri* capable of serious head-hunting to add to his growing arsenal of edged weapons. After a short conversation with the master knife maker, Thornton dropped the phone back onto its cradle, nodding to Silver, who was admiring one of Tanaka's ancient suits of Japanese armor.

"I take it the man's awaiting our presence?" inquired Jason as he thanked Tanaka for the day's beating.

"Yeah. Phill's closed the shop so we'll have his full attention. He said he's pulled a coupla things out from his private inventory, based upon what Tanaka told him we might be looking for when the appointment was set up. It's gonna take about an hour to get over there, given the L.A. traffic this time of the day, so we'd better get moving.''

Tanaka-san escorted them down to the lobby, where they agreed on a time for the next day's instruction. ''Phill is expensive,'' he reminded both men, ''but his prices are fair and his work is pure. What he will show you is meant to be used, make no mistake about that. I will be interested to see what you select when you return tomorrow.'' With that he bowed slightly and left them standing on the sidewalk, the roar of going-home traffic enveloping them in a symphony of automobile harmonics.

Halfway across town the Corvette's phone announced an incoming call. Snatching the receiver from its leather-lined pocket atop the padded dash, Bo growled a hello while deftly missing a taxi that skidded across two lanes of traffic in hopes of snatching up an unwary passenger.

''What the hell you two doing in Los Angeles? Linda told me you'd blown out of town for a few days and gave me the Hyatt's number in North Hollywood. Thinking of getting into the movies or what?''

Calvin Bailey's voice brought a smile to Thornton's face even though he knew the cross-country call meant there was a mission in the works for his team. Bailey, a former SEAL, was Thornton's contact inside the DEA where SPRINGBLADE was concerned. A highly classified covert ops project, SPRINGBLADE exercised a presidential sanction to carry out direct action strikes against immediate threats to the nation's security. Through the person of Conrad Billings, a senior field chief for the DEA, Bailey received the Oval Office's directives, which activated the SPRINGBLADE option.

"Cut the crap, squid. If you'll kick on your scrambler, I'll do the same here and we can talk. You're like a kid in college. You never call unless you need something." With a flick of his right index finger Thornton powered up the latest mobile scrambler, which Bailey had ordered sent out after the team's foray into Nicaragua. Capable of multiple band mixing, the scrambler allowed the team's One-Zero to discuss upcoming operations wherever either Billings or Bailey might catch him, the 'vette's mobile phone never far from the night warrior's hand.

"You there?" It was Bailey, who'd flipped his own unit on back in Washington, D.C., where he was posted as a "special operative" to the drug czar's staff, although only Bennent actually knew what the man did for the president in terms of the Administration's "black" policy on both internal and external threats.

Thornton wheeled the maximum sports car onto the freeway heading toward Garden Grove, an appreciative glance thrown his way by a very foxy redhead whose own set of wheels looked every bit as impressive from where the former Green Beret sat. Torquing the machine up to sixty, Bo settled back into his custom-stitched black leather seat, the phone tucked up under his chin. "Go. I've got you five-by and Silver's sitting next to me counting his money already. Whatta you got for us?"

"Ever heard of General Duc Phong? Used to be C-in-C of the Golden Tiger Division back in the bad old days of Vietnam?"

Bo nodded to himself, the man's face popping into his mental viewer from a hundred years ago. "Sure. Phong was considered a top field commander even by our standards. His division kicked the VC out of his zone of responsibility, then went after the NVA when they tried to retake the lost ground. He was one of the few stars in the South Vietnamese army as I recall.''

''Well, that 'star' appears to be getting tarnished from what our intell reports confirm. Phong got out in '75, brought most of his family and staff with him just before Saigon fell. He settled in Taos, New Mexico, and looked to be just another senior military official who decided to make America his home. Naturally he didn't have much problem financing his resettlement, Agency records strongly supporting our own show the general was running some very profitable enterprises out of his command bunker during the hostilities.''

Bo snorted. ''That shouldn't surprise anyone. Most of the Victs had a little 'something' going on the sidelines regardless of their rank. What was Phong into, dope? Money? Guns?''

''The general was providing armed escorts for Southeast Asian dope lords running their caravans in and out of South Vietnam. Over a period of about five years he became quite influential, to the point of purchasing hundreds of acres of the best opium producing land dirty money could buy. It seems he holds an impressive amount of 'stock' in several different countries, including Cambodia, Thailand, and Burma.

''That sounds more like SLAM country to me,'' interjected Thornton as the redhead pulled up alongside them again, her window as well as her top down. The retired SF'er was highly impressed with what the woman possessed as far as serious-business boobs went, acknowledging so with a hearty smile and a ''thumbs up'' gesture with his free hand. With a roar, the low-slung Porche left the Corvette behind, Silver saying something about life in the big city as he punched up a traffic report on the car's stereo system.

Bailey's voice re-registered inside Thornton's head, the big-titted Valley girl's exhibition history as the German speed machine turned off and headed for Venice Beach. ''. . . Bannion's team has been doing some balls-to-the-wall interdiction in Burma lately, and his reports mention a stateside connection which is probably Phong. That's where SPRINGBLADE comes in.''

Switching lanes, Thornton eased back on the pedal, dropping the Corvette's speed to just under the posted fifty-five limit. ''How so?'' he asked, looking for his own exit, which he knew was coming up quickly.

''Over the last six months we've been finding the remains of fired-up drug smugglers scattered across Arizona, California, and New Mexico. Almost every incident displays the same m.o., preset ambushes with lots of firepower and no survivors. Most if not all of the caravans use mules to transport their loads across the border, and in every instance we've found their pack trays stripped of whatever cargo was on board before the hit went down.

''Intell coming from our deep cover people in Mexico tells us there's a major rift which has developed between the Latin cartels and the Southeast Asian tongs. Interdiction is having an effect on supply; supply, naturally, having an effect on pricing. The Latins are attempting to import huge volumes of cocaine and heroin into the country to make up for the recent super-seizures we've made, and to offset the volume being handled by the Asians . . .''

Thornton interrupted the fast-talking narc, a tiny ember deep within his brain beginning to burst into flames as the story unfolded. ''Which they can easily do based upon their proximity to the United States as opposed to our oriental friends across the pond, right?''

"Roger that," confirmed Bailey. "The Asians have to necessarily move smaller loads because the risk of their being interdicted is so high. Smaller loads means higher prices due to a greater overhead because you have to ship more shit to maintain the current consumption levels.

"What we believe is happening is a major rip-off of the Latin Connection's shipments by one General Duc Phong. Because of the crossover in product, somebody in one of the major drug producing countries who is in a position to compromise Latino transactions is doing so. The boys from Down South put up the cash, take the risk of getting into their system, moving it across the border into Gringolandia . . ."

". . . where General Phong lowers the boom on the runners, plowing nothing but pure profit back into the proverbial oriental coffer."

On the other end Calvin laughed at Thornton's immediate grasp of the situation. "You've seen this movie before, eh?"

Laughing himself, Bo responded. "Yeah, nothing ever changes. We used to watch this kinda shit taking place when it came to weapons, medical supplies, construction material, you name it. The Viets were grand masters of the retail trade game, and this sounds like something they'd delight in being a part of."

Suddenly serious, Bailey made his request. Thornton's team wasn't tied into doing the government's business anytime King George called. Bo had reserved the right to "Just Say No" anytime he felt the job was not in line with the big man's thinking. "I'd like to fly out to L.A. and meet with you on this one. Billings feels we've got to make a grand slam play on both Phong and a mover down Mexico way by the name of Canales. He'd like

SPRINGBLADE to take the contract, and of course the
president has given his blessing *if* you'll accept the offer.''

Thornton caught the Garden Grove exit as it came up,
deftly popping the Corvette into the far right turn lane
so they could get up to Hartsfield's shop, which was only
a few blocks away. ''To be honest, Cal, this kinda sounds
more like a Border Patrol/DEA operation than something
we should get involved in. Even the FBI could mount
*something*, give 'em a chance to use those new 10mm
hand cannons they just bought.''

Bailey nodded to himself, knowing he'd have to use
his ace-in-the-hole to pull Thornton in. He hated doing
so, but Billings had made it clear there was no time to
attempt putting together a joint task force. ''Border Patrol
officers found a body dump in New Mexico last week,''
he began. ''Buncha gunslingers got wasted along with
fifteen or so mules. We figure some serious shit got ripped
off by Phong's people, given the size of the packs the
animals were carrying.

''One of the dead smugglers was a Mexican who we've
got very little information on other than he was a midlevel
enforcer for Canales. When we found his body, there
was a beret alongside it. The name tag inside said it
belonged to an active duty SF captain who was a TAC-
adviser to one of your outfit's reserve teams. This team
totally disappeared some time ago while taking part in a
classified border watch operation. We figure this Mex
and some of Canales's boys whacked them somewhere
out in the desert. We never found the bodies.''

There was silence on the other end, only the sound of
a radio and the 'vette's low growl as it inched its way
up a busy street somewhere on the West Coast. When
Thornton's voice materialized, it was as hard and low as

Bailey had ever heard it. "Make a reservation at the Hyatt on Sunset. Leave your flight information at the front desk with Lonnie, fly into LAX, where we'll pick you up in a rental. When can you be here?"

"Late tomorrow afternoon. Conrad's putting a package together for me to bring out. Profiles, background, the whole program. You read it over, we talk, you say what goes. Deal?"

Silver tapped Thornton's shoulder, pointing to a tasteful sign announcing Hartsfield's business. Thornton pulled the car into a side street, letting the engine rumble for a moment before turning it off. The silence inside the Corvette was tangible, broken only by Bo as he closed the phone link between Calvin and himself. "If Phong and his people are involved, that's one thing. If it was Canales whose dirt balls knocked off the captain and his people, *his* balls belong to me! Deal?"

Bailey squeezed his eyes shut, knowing he'd have to give Thornton what he wanted or lose the team's involvement. It would have to be between Bailey and the angry One-Zero on the other end; Billings couldn't sanction a fish as big as Canales going down on nothing more than a personal vendetta. "Deal!" was all the young narc said, then the line went dead with an audible *snap* as Thornton hung up.

Letting out a long overheld breath of stale oxygen, Bailey punched his intercom's button, hearing his secretary's voice on the other end. "Get me airborne, Marty. Front row seating on the first thing smoking to L.A. Call the Hyatt on Sunset, get me on the same floor as a 'Mr. B. Thornton.' Buzz me back when you've set it all up, charge everything to Mr. Billing's card number."

Bailey grunted as his gal Friday repeated his request word for word. Spinning around in his chair, the former

SEAL lit a fresh Marlboro from the half-empty pack, blowing a double stream of gray smoke from his nostrils. Los Angeles in time for dinner, he mused. He hoped Bo had a room overlooking the city, which was Calvin's favorite on the West Coast. Tomorrow night he'd help one of the fiercest combat soldiers he'd ever met plan the eventual termination of two parasites, men whose style of living was fueled by dope.

Los Angeles was a fitting place to put such a business deal together, he thought, as his intercom began buzzing like a trapped fly on his desk.

# CHAPTER

**3**

Duc Phong stood alone on his balcony. Inside the spacious office he kept in his home, men were moving about, carrying large cardboard boxes filled with the plastic-wrapped rewards of their last raid. The general was in heavy thought, the contents of a FAX message from an old and trusted colleague still living in Taiwan troubling him. It seemed one of the *dinky-dau* Colombians had discovered Phong's involvement in the series of devastating drug rip-offs that had been taking place. The man had issued a contract with the general's name on it, and it was only by luck that Duc's friend had come upon the information. The community of drug traders was quite small at the top, with secrecy among thieves as scarce a commodity as honesty.

Phong knew the only way to cancel his death sentence was to levy one himself. Time, as always, was of the essence. From Taiwan the general knew the Colombian was vacationing at sea, soon to make port near Fort Walton Beach, Florida, where he would take on fuel and provisions. Phong had already alerted his security staff, issuing instructions that left little doubt as to what was to happen when the hit team sent from Colombia was discovered in Taos. It was a big desert. Now what concerned the former Vietnamese officer was who to send to Florida. The team would not be large, perhaps three men at the most. There would have to be an old-timer in charge, someone whose abilities were proven when it came to wet work. The other two men could be drawn from the new breed of soldier Phong was developing. They were primarily the sons and daughters of those soldiers he'd gathered around him after leaving Vietnam in 1975, eager to do his bidding as repayment for his kindness and protection as they settled in America.

It was this devotion that Phong preyed upon, perverting his charges' sense of honor and loyalty so that the general's criminal activities could be carried out. The latest enterprise was code-named "Phu Dung," or Phoenix. Like the mythical bird, Duc Phong was rising out of the ashes of defeat, establishing his reign and extending his control through the use of terror and murder. The Phoenix project was the general's most ambitious yet, involving over a hundred men to carry out. The richness of the fields to be tilled was Phong's greatest motivator, and his enemy one whose losses would garner no sympathy from the current Administration.

Duc Phong hadn't started out as a criminal. During the long war his country fought he'd risen through the officer ranks quickly, his reputation as a combat officer bringing him to the attention of the Americans who were supporting South Vietnam's efforts to remain free. Phong became one of the youngest generals to be commissioned, and he took the title seriously. His division soon began chalking up impressive victories against the Viet Cong, forcing them to give ground and finally throwing them out of the general's TAOR completely. Then the NVA came in, intent on winning back an area they believed was rightfully theirs. The fighting had been harsh against the irregular forces of the VC; against the NVA it was brutal. Phong pulled out all the stops, rooting the enemy out wherever there was a rumor of his presence. Those civilians who supported the North's troops, regardless of their motivation, were rounded up and moved completely out of the combat zone. Others, whose loyalty to the South was less than satisfactory as ordained by the general's hard-charging S-2 shop, were executed. Phong himself labored endlessly with his American advisors, using every tactic he knew to ensure a constant flow of arms, ammunition, and air power to his troops in the field. It came, primarily because the general was a minority among his peers when it came to providing actual combat results. Phong realized this and used it both as a velvet glove, and a steel hammer when needing an extra lift of Hueys or a few hundred more rounds of 105 for the guns.

The NVA soon realized that they would only regain control of the situation if Phong was removed from his command on a permanent basis. Assassination teams were formed and sent forth, their orders to kill the general wherever he might be found. Again, Phong's intelligence arm proved to be his saving grace. As often as not it was the NVA hitmen's heads that were found spiked to the trail, "Gold Tiger" shoulder patches, with white general's stars embroidered in their centers, stapled into the dead men's foreheads. Phong's division succeeded in smashing the NVA's effort to uproot them, the bloodied remnants of Uncle Ho's forces fleeing across a neutral border to escape the wrath of the Tiger's claws.

Now he was being threatened again. Duc Phong had been able to bring more than most to his adopted country. Still, his funds were few and the exiled general had found life in America hard to adjust to. He remembered blanching when reading about one of his peers opening a liquor store in Los Angeles. A liquor store! The man had once been the cream of the army, a favorite of the American press corps! Now he was no more than a lowly clerk, his medals hung behind a cash register to be ogled by drunks.

Phong had moved to New Mexico for the climate, buying several acres of land with what he'd brought out of the South and building a stout home in which to live. Phong watched as his countrymen attempted to escape the slaughter which the communists were carrying out, heeding no outcry from the exalted "world community" as they rid Saigon and the surrounding cities and towns of disruptive elements. In America he saw the subtle shadow of discrimination raise its head as thousands of Vietnamese attempted to immigrate. Phong conveniently forgot how his race had conspired against the Rhade and other mountain tribesmen of Vietnam, ignoring their call for equality and crushing their attempt to become free men. Instead he saw only the insult to the Vietnamese people by fat, dumb, and happy Americans who had never had to fight for their country, not to mention a meal. He had been outraged, then saddened, and finally moved to an anger that birthed Phu Dung.

It had not been difficult to draw together his forces. As the word raced through the many Vietnamese communities of General Duc Phong's invitation to join him in New Mexico, hundreds responded. Phong carefully selected only those who had experienced no success after leaving their homeland. Most were ex-soldiers, having no other skills than those the army had taught them. Skills that did them no good when it came to earning a daily wage on the streets of America, but skills that General Phong understood and appreciated as they applied to his daring plan to cash in on the Latino drug trade. In the end, Phong gathered around him a combat-ready force of loyal former comrades-in-arms. Careful diplomacy opened the doors to the powerful Southeast Asian cartels, cartels raging their own battles against the competitors in Central and South America. Of course they would help the respected general, whose goals were not in conflict with their own.

And so the raids began.

"General?"

At the sound of his title Phong returned from where his mind had been wandering, fixing the young man who had approached him with a tolerant grin. If anyone thought the Vietnamese to be frightened of his enemies, they were dead wrong. He was a combat officer, trained and bloodied on the gory fields of battle. Phong thrived on the challenge of staying alive, of winning regardless of the sacrifice or loss. The Colombian was used to killing unprotected judges and noisy politicians. His reputation was built upon the corpses of nickel-dime street pushers and half-cocked gunmen. What he was facing was a professional in the arts of command and decision. Phong would deliver a stinging blow to the tin-pot dope lord's empire, sending a message to his *compañeros* regardless of their nationality or power base. Send an assassin after the Golden Tiger himself? Hadn't the VC tried that? Hadn't the cream of the NVA attempted to follow suit? The Colombian's death would announce Phong's policy about being threatened, a policy none would have any doubts about.

"Yes, Mike. Is Diem inside yet?" Phong hoped the old sergeant had arrived; he needed to get things moving now that his decision had been made.

"Yes. The old man is waiting in your office, a bag packed down in one of the cars. Will Diem be leaving this morning?" Mike was one of the new generation, a favorite of Phong's and hence a trusted lieutenant in the organization. He had made several daring strikes along the Arizona border, liberating well over fifteen million dollars in drugs and laundered cash from the well-laden caravans crossing the border at will.

Phong strode across the hand-set tiles of the balcony's decking. Although in his fifties, the general was lean and as hard as he'd been twenty years before. A runner since coming to New Mexico, the Vietnamese pounded out ten miles a day across the desert's face, a select team of bodyguards on point, at the flanks, and bringing up the rear as protection against attack. Underneath the enlarged home, Phong had built a complete indoor shooting range both as a training center for his men and as a diversion for himself. The range also doubled as a courtroom for those who violated the strict rules that governed the general's New Mexican domain. "Yes. You will drive him and those he chooses to the airport. Make sure my old friend has enough cash to make their journey comfortable; issue him one of the company's credit cards as well. I'll want hotel reservations made for Diem in Florida, a car also. You will see to it?"

Mike nodded. He knew Sergeant Diem had been with the general for years, serving with him in Vietnam during the war, then following him to America after the fall. Diem was a legendary figure to the men who served Duc

Phong. He had graduated from the Vietnamese ranger school, going on to win his American jump wings at the in-country school run by the Special Forces. An impressive combat career followed, with the rugged Vietnamese going on to take part in long-range reconnaissance operations and, finally, becoming one of the original members of the famed Provisional Reconnaissance Unit, or PRU. If the general was sending Diem out, it meant someone somewhere was going to die, thought Mike.

Phong entered his office, seeing Diem sitting comfortably in one of the deep leather chairs scattered about the room. As the general approached him, Diem rose, holding out his hand, which Phong took, shaking warmly. "How are you, you old water buffalo?" asked Duc.

"Well, General. You have need of an old sergeant's skills I hear. Where is it you want me to go, and what do you need accomplished?"

Phong gestured for Diem to once again be seated, taking his own chair behind the heavy teak desk, which he'd brought with him from his headquarters in the South. Opening a drawer, Phong removed a long, thin cigarette. Wetting its entire length between his moistened lips, Duc lit the hand-rolled smoke, drawing its sweet aroma deep into his lungs. Exhaling slowly, Phong allowed the delicate tickle of the opium to begin its journey to his brain. He enjoyed relaxing this way, especially in light of the successes he had enjoyed over the last several weeks. Fixing Diem with a warm smile, Phong began. "We have stung our Latin 'friends' well, taking several caravans out from under them in both New Mexico and Arizona. Our own organization has been most adroit in pumping the results of our attentions into the pipeline at

our disposal, with profits most impressive. You are aware
of the death threat made against me?''

Diem nodded, a wave of his hand indicating he wasn't
too concerned with a threat made before the action itself
took place. Diem believed you struck first, then announced your victory.

Phong continued, a second lungful of high-grade opium lifting toward the alabaster ceiling. ''This Colombian
is a close associate of the Mexican Canales. He wishes
to make a statement to his cartel's membership, as well
as to those of our friends in Southeast Asia. I do not
intend to fulfill his desire for my demise, and so I am
sending you to settle our difference.

''You may choose two of your best soldiers. Mike is
arranging where you will stay as well as transportation.
Funding will be provided before you leave.'' Reaching
into a half-open drawer at his side, the Vietnamese removed a sealed envelope, roughly the size of a pocket
novel. With a slight toss he sent it Diem's way, the
package deftly caught by the smiling sergeant as he enjoyed the game both men were playing.

''Our intelligence section has been hard at work I take
it?''

Phong laughed, the sound light and harmonious.
''Your target folder is complete. The primary has taken
a long voyage since issuing my 'death sentence,' obviously hoping to stay out of harm's way until the deed
is done. The S-2 has discovered they will dock at Fort
Walton, in Florida, in three days' time.

''It is my wish that the Colombian be taught a lesson.
Do not make his death secretive, nor allow it to be blamed
upon the gods. As they say here in America, 'put on a
show.' Make sure the press's thirst for ratings is well
met.''

Diem nodded. "We will need certain items, and weapons of course." Waiting for Phong's answer, the hardcore Vietnamese ranger played gently with a handcrafted ivory Buddha hanging on a slender thread of spun gold around his neck.

"We have a strong population base in Miami. I'll see to it our people there know of your coming and are prepared to support whatever needs you may have. I do not need to tell you, Diem, this will be a difficult assignment. The Colombian will be alert, he will have prepared well for his own safety.

"Phu Dung has proven a most successful enterprise for us. We have struck the Latins hard, killing many of their best couriers and enriching our coffers by millions of dollars. The Drug Enforcement Agency runs from firestorm to firestorm, both confused and perhaps privately appreciative that someone is carrying out an action they themselves are prevented from taking.

"Still, the time is coming when we ourselves will be moved against. Canales is in Mexico, and he must move quickly if his organization is to hold on to power there. Your strike against his link with the brotherhood in Colombia and Bolivia will accomplish three things of importance to Phu Dung. Do you know what they are, my friend?"

Diem dropped the tiny statue back beneath his shirt. "You will be safe, General. With this man dead, the contract he has issued will die with him. What more could we want than this?"

Duc laughed in appreciation of his noncom's directness and simple assessment. Diem was a soldier, dedicated to carrying out a soldier's tasks. Politics for him was a game played with paper, not guns. "Well spoken and quite true, Sergeant. My personal well-being will once again be assured, although I do not seek that goal alone.

"Of equal importance will be the message our Latin competitors will receive when word of their *compañeros's* death reaches them. They will realize we are a force to be taken seriously, a force capable and willing to use the bomb and the bullet to ensure our domination of their heretofore unchallenged domain.

"Also, Canales will be isolated, cut off from the rest, whose distrust of him will only be fed by the suspicion he may have betrayed the Colombian for his own ends. When the time is right, when Canales is weakened and cast adrift by his allies in Central America, then Phu Dung will lop his head off and spike it along the border for all to see!"

Diem rose, bowing slightly in respect to his lord. "With your permission I will take the Trung brothers with me. They performed extremely well during our last ambush and both are exceptional marksmen with the rocket."

With a wave of his hand, Phong released the two men to Diem's control. "Go now. Whatever you need, ask for it in my name. Walk carefully among our enemies, remembering one need not fear the known foe, only the unknown adversary. I await your successful return with eager ears."

Diem turned and left as quietly as he had entered the air-conditioned office. Alone, Duc Phong finished his smoke, then slipped back into the chair from which he'd made a thousand command decisions over the years.

The Colombian was as good as dead, of this there was no doubt. Diem would weave a strong net around the man when he arrived in Florida, the sergeant's mention of using the Trungs' skill with rocket launchers a sure sign of what was to come. Now the general needed to begin pondering what would come afterward, what moves and countermoves his powerful enemies might take against him. His network in Southeast Asia was tight, their interests parallel to his own when it came to clashing with the smugglers of South America. Which reminded him of his latest FAX from Thailand.

It seemed U.S. agents along with Burmese troops had struck yet again at one of the major drug transfer points inside that country. His report detailed the many dead (there was no report of any wounded, not surprising to Phong, who understood the reality of total war) and the tremendous loss of product at the hands of the invading force. This was the third such attack led by American drug commandos in as many months, and there was worry their success would become a flood tide, threatening existing routes and safe havens throughout the much-talked-about "Golden Triangle."

Phong made a mental note to keep himself abreast of the situation, although there was little he could do from where he sat except lend advice. Coming to his feet, the now-stoned drug warlord allowed his glazed eyes to travel over the many pictures and awards that were hung with care from his walls. Dead comrades and smiling allies, blood-red ribbons for valor and brilliant gold medals for honor, they were all there. General Duc Phong nodded to himself as each memory cascaded across his silent inner screen. The old days were the glory days, he thought. The present was the result of tragic wrongs levied against him and his people by powers they couldn't control. What was left was an opportunity to make whatever the Golden Tiger himself could of a bitter situation.

"Phu Dung," he muttered aloud. Phu Dung would be the means by which at least one group of disenfranchised refugees would make their way in a hostile and uncon-

cerned land. ''Phu Dung!'' he exclaimed to the heavens
held captive under the ceiling of his spacious office. Phu
Dung.

Phoenix. A war bird rising from the ashes of its own
defeat. A project carried out in the South to dismantle
and annihilate the Viet Cong infrastructure. A project of
assassins and patriots from both sides.

Phu Dung. Phoenix. They were the same then, today,
and always.

# CHAPTER

**▅▅▅▅▅▅**

# 4

Two days later Sergeant Diem lowered his Steiner field glasses, a satisfied look smeared across his scarred face. He and the Trungs had flown directly into Miami, where Diem had met with members of a Vietnamese veterans' group handsomely supported by the general. There were several former comrades-in-arms present, lending a sense of homecoming to the otherwise strictly business meeting. Diem had made his plans for the Colombian's assassination during the long flight from Taos. Where others might casually sketch out a day at the beach, or a night on the town, Diem amused himself by plotting the death of his commanding officer's enemy.

Death was not new to the former PRU noncom. He'd been trained to deliver it with all the force of a B-40 rocket. The war had been going on since the sergeant's childhood, with foreign invaders/supporters stomping through the country's jungles and mountains like elephants on a rampage. The army was a natural step for the young man, whose village was so poor not even the Viet Cong troubled themselves with it. Life in the army might be dangerous, but at least you got fed and clothed. On a more selfish note, you were also given a gun, and guns were power in a country struggling for its future.

Death, thought Diem as the younger Trung appeared beside him, a cold bottle of Coke in his hands. Death was a solution to problems without solutions. He'd taken quickly to the caliber of warfare practiced by the elite recon units being trained by the Americans and their allies. Diem was one of his country's tigers, a fighter who gloried in taking it straight up the enemy's behind with no holds barred. In time his battlefield exploits and coolness under fire earned him a "black" recommendation to take part in a program called "Phoenix." Diem leapt at the opportunity and was given a team in the newly formed Provisional Recon Unit, or PRU, force formed to support Phoenix's operations.

The goal of the program was to dismantle the Viet Cong infrastructure within the South. Several methods were used, to include assassination if all else failed. Diem thought the concept fitting. The VC had been waging their own form of Phoenix for years, murdering thousands of village chiefs, teachers, religious men, and government supporters without mercy or publicity. As the Green Berets who were some of Diem's instructors said, "What goes around comes around . . . ," and in this case it was so. Hundreds of VC cadre were informed upon by those whom they were attempting to subvert, with PRU teams rounding them up and carting them off so that government control could once again be established in a relative peace. Some of the VC ended up dead, but not as many as claimed in the rumors began by the communists. Phoenix was a success up until the enemy realized their own table had been turned, then it was a war of propaganda, lies, and allegations, which the communists could not be beaten at.

After the dissolution of Phoenix, Diem transferred to recon and became one of the few Vietnamese to run missions with some of the most secretive of the special projects launched during the war. He had changed, though, realizing the South could not win and that the Americans were doomed to leave just as had the Chinese, Japanese, British, and French. So Diem fought for the pure joy of losing himself in battle. He became an extraordinary killing machine, well versed in the art of rendering another man useless. After a while it mattered not which unit he was with, under whose command he followed orders, or where the war was fought. Until he met General Duc Phong, and then life once again had meaning.

"We have the photos taken yesterday, Diem. They are quite good, as you thought they would be. When shall we examine them?"

His companion's question reeled Diem back into the present, all thoughts of life in Vietnam's death struggle vanquished as he faced the serious Vietnamese standing next to him. "Now is as good a time as any. Is your brother at the hotel on watch?"

Vo Trung nodded, gesturing to the multi-story hotel perched on the beach's edge like a sprinter in the blocks. "He has been watching the boat all morning as ordered. The Colombian has appeared only twice, to talk with members of the crew who are hurrying to get them back out to sea. Refueling was accomplished by 1000 hours; they wait only for provisions."

Diem smiled at a passing tourist, bobbing his head in

the accepted manner that foreigners believed common
for any Oriental. He was playing his own game with the
ignorant cow, knowing she would never remember him
if questioned after the attack took place. After all, we
all look alike don't we? The thought broadened Diem's
smile so that Vo began laughing, thinking the grizzled
veteran was lusting after the corpulent pig on two legs.

Ten minutes later both men sat comfortably in the
living room of their luxury suite, a splay of black and
white enlargements laced across the low wooden coffee
table between them. Diem was the uncontested team
leader for the mission, his trigger finger tracing a trajec-
tory for one of the Trung brothers' LAW rockets from
a second-story fast-food joint directly into the hull of the
Colombian's boat. The group chattered in Vietnamese
among themselves, a second rocket site selected for Vo's
brother Liu, who would fire his antitank weapon first, in
hopes of driving the primary target off the seventy-five-
foot floating palace and onto the open space of the
bleached white wooden dock.

It would be there where Diem would personally kill
him.

Late afternoon arrived, its sun an orange boiling thing,
which radiated hotly as it began sinking into the ocean.
Traffic was dense as business owners began closing up
shop, tourists hurrying for their condos and motel rooms
to freshen up for an early dinner and night on the town.
From where he lay on his belly behind the balcony's
stone facade, Diem easily watched Vo Trung as the man
crossed the street from their hotel, a long blue-and-gold
gym bag draped across his right shoulder. Inside the bag
was a fully extended and armed LAW rocket, stolen from
the ranger base at Camp Darby a year before.

Diem watched in admiration as the young Vietnamese

smiled and chatted with idle tourists stuck in the middle of the street as thousands of pounds of wheeled steel cruised by them. Vo had learned the sergeant's lessons well, understanding his own survival was of the utmost importance when carrying out a mission such as theirs. Vo was playing his role perfectly, a tourist in Florida out for a late afternoon walk, perhaps a visit to the gym for a light workout. He drew no attention to himself by either deed or word. No one but Vo's brother and Diem knew of the long-bladed Western hunting knife held tightly between Vo's hip and his belted Levis, a long-tailed shirt concealing the leather handle. Both brothers were skilled bladesmen, taught personally by Diem, who'd learned his craft with a knife the old-fashioned way. As with everything else, they'd each purchased a knife of their own choosing in Miami before driving to Fort Walton. Diem had forbidden handguns, wanting no one on his team to feel he could afford a face-to-face confrontation during the strike. A knife was a weapon of last resort, an ace-high should the shit hit the fan.

Vo completed his short journey, and waving good-bye to his street-bound friends, he entered a short alley, where he then disappeared. Minutes later he appeared on the roof of the hamburger joint, stripping off his shirt and laying out a towel on which he then stretched out. If anyone was watching, they would assume Vo was catching some late afternoon rays. Diem alone noted the gym bag's position next to the low wall overlooking the dock. He knew its mouth was wide open, the LAW primed and ready to be launched against the exposed aft section of the yacht.

Liu had been in position for nearly a half hour, his attack point located in the far corner of a nearly deserted pay parking lot. He was sitting on a cement breakwater

that separated the beach from the cracked paving of the
lot, a Sony Walkman in his hand, its headset clamped
firmly around his skull. Liu's LAW was also hidden away
in the depths of a tote bag, this one vivid in its decoration.
After firing, Liu would drop off the wall onto the beach
and make his way toward the string of T-shirt shops and
jewelry stores located at the south end of the block. Diem
would see neither of the two brothers until they rejoined
as a group later that night in one of the shopping malls
located outside the gates of Eglin Air Force Base.

Secure in the knowledge that his supporting fires were
in position, Diem busied himself with his end of the
operation. It would be up to him to seal the Colombian's
fate, a hat trick that would require split-second timing
and a steady eye. Among Diem's many talents were those
of a sniper. He prided himself on his ability to hit a man
full in the face at five hundred meters with open sights,
a thousand if the gun was scoped. Back in Taos, the
Vietnamese practiced his hobby out in the arid desert
behind the general's home, often firing for hours as his
charges replaced man-sized targets at a regular pace.

For this removal, which is how Diem thought of his
job, the sergeant had chosen to use a Ruger M-77 6mm
bolt gun. He'd shipped the weapon to his Miami contact
via overnight express, picking it up once the team had
landed and been moved to their safehouse. The heavy
wooden stock had been removed, replaced by a fiberglass
hunting stock in a forest-green camouflage pattern. The
rifle's action had been worked by Diem himself until the
trigger pull equaled two and one-half pounds. He'd then
scoped the system with a 3X-9X32 wide-angle tube from
Timber King. A simple, black nylon sling hung from the
integral hooks built into the stock, so that Diem could
snug the rifle up into the pocket of his shoulder when

sighting in. It was a competent interdiction system, inexpensive, reliable, and flat-shooting.

Diem preferred the 6mm round for its velocity and accuracy when used in urban or built-up areas. For this occasion he elected to use Remington's 100-grain CORE-LOKT soft points, liking their expansion and knowing they'd blow through the Colombian's bone structure without a thought. Once inside the cranium, free to run amok among the millions of startled brain cells, the bullet would mushroom like a spring flower. *If* the round exited, it would take a section of skull with it the size of a tennis ball. Should it stay inside . . . well, Diem knew what churned gruel looked like.

The shot would be difficult, given that the target would most likely be moving erratically, stunned by the force of the explosions around him and beginning to panic when he realized where he was. Diem wanted to drop the man dead-center of the dock so his body would be quickly located by the police and media. Although the Vietnamese marksman prided himself on his ability to make one-shot kills, he would ensure the Colombian's death by firing a second bullet into an exposed vital area once the man was down. There would be no one else in the Colombian's party shot, a message to all of exactly who had been the target from the moment hostilities opened.

In preparation the sergeant built a low base on which to rest his rifle's forestock so that all its weight would be off the shooter. Only an inch or so of the lightweight barrel protruded past the lip of the balcony, with Diem's prone body well back in the shadows of the overhang above him. The sliding glass door was open so he could exit quickly if it became necessary, but more so the sniper could rapidly recover the rifle, rolling back into the empty room as soon as the second shot was let loose, its impact verified. No fuss, no muss. Everyone's attention would be on the burning boat once the first of the rockets slammed into it, Diem counting on the sound of the fuel tanks' exploding to cover what little *pop* his rifle would make once he engaged the Colombian.

Glancing at his Rolex Presidential, a gift from the general for a particularly healthy haul from a recent caravan, Diem noted it was nearing time for Liu to commence his portion of the assault. Vo would fire his LAW sixty seconds later, giving the Colombian time to assess his predicament before blowing out the rear of the low-slung sailboat. Their target's cabin was located in the bow, aluminum stairs leading from its private entrance atop the deck to the dock below. He would have no trouble getting out should that be his decision, one which Diem had no doubt he would make. From there, it was a headlong rush up the dockway toward the gated entrance to the marina. Peering through his scope, the Vietnamese smiled at how well they'd chosen their hotel room. From his vantage point Diem's barrel looked right down Death's alley, an easy shot for someone with the Viet's eye. He'd let the man reach the halfway point so the body wouldn't experience too much charring once the yacht blew. The fire department would be on the scene within minutes anyhow, so a positive ID wouldn't be much in question.

Rotating the rifle's bolt upward, he slipped the well-cared-for mechanism rearward, jacking a shiny new round into the breech and securing it in place with a subtle shove of the bolt forward. He'd placed one of the bed's covers on the hard cement of the balcony's flooring, lying on it with his right leg cocked at a forty-five–degree angle. Ensuring the weapon's safety was in the ''ON'' posture, Diem scoped out the yacht once more, using the scope's intense magnification to his advantage. Satisfied with the routine taking place on deck, the Viet's shoulders hunched upward involuntarily as the explosive wallop of Liu's LAW being fired punctured the afternoon sounds.

He lay his cheek against the warm fiberglass of the rifle's stock and began taking up the slack under his curling finger. Out of the corner of his eye he caught the booster-powered flight of the LAW as it streaked across the narrow expanse of sand and water, arcing slightly upward and then slamming headlong into the tin-and-wood motorboat shed perched on the corner of the dock. The resulting explosion ignited gasoline fumes that had built up inside the repair facility, causing an even greater display of fireworks as the building's walls and roof flew apart in a hot gush of splintered steel and wood.

From his vantage point Diem observed at least three of the Colombian's crew die as a wash of searing fragments collided with their unprotected bodies. The sound of the explosion was enormous, stopping traffic on the street and dropping people to the sidewalks as it rolled like an angry wheel over them. A minute later Vo's rocket was in flight. This time the yacht itself was the target, the anti-armor seeker roaring off the rooftop where Vo knelt, still shirtless, and into the aft panel of the boat. The thick hull proved no match for the LAW, which punched its way inside the engine compartment like a hot poker into plastic. The warhead careened off one of the large diesel engines, impacting a half-second later against the bulkhead. A fireball erupted inside the boat, long tongues of evil flame blowing through the narrow passageway leading up into the boat's lavish interior. Two more of the crew were incinerated, another knocked unconscious under the one-two punch coming from the two Vietnamese rocket men.

Diem had already swung the rifle's barrel toward the bow, where the first of the Colombian's guests staggered up onto the foredeck. He was a lean, handsome man, immediately recognizable as a semi-important congressman from the Midwest. Half-dressed, the man slipped in his bare feet and landed hard on the deck, causing Diem to smile slightly. How would Congressman Perfect explain his presence on a bombed-out yacht owned by a dead Colombian drug smuggler, he thought. It would be interesting to hear on the evening's news. A second form appeared in Diem's scope, this time a young woman. She was half-dressed, naked from the waist up. Her well-formed breasts jiggled from side to side as she scampered over the dazed form of the politician, her painted mouth open in an unheard scream. Long legs led upward to a sheath of bright yellow nylon, which housed her hips, also most impressive. The Colombian's girlfriend? Or perhaps a "constituent" of the congressman . . . ? No matter, thought the sniper as he awaited his target.

Diem caught the single brown hand as it clenched at the stainless steel railing, the powerful bulk of the Colombian lurching up into the open as a secondary explosion tore through the yacht's guts. A strong southern breeze was in Diem's favor, blowing dark oily smoke from the combined fires away from the burning hull and out to sea. Locking the cross hairs onto the man, Diem watched as the Colombian shouted something back down the gangway. Yet another blast from inside the hull shook the boat, dropping the Colombian painfully to his knees. The girl latched onto his back, her face now contorted into one long, raging scream of fear. Diem watched as the man struggled to throw her off, finally grabbing a

handful of thick brown hair and wrenching her forward
so she landed hard on her back on the deck. With a single
chop, he caught the woman squarely across the throat,
cracking her larynx as if it were cheap glass. Diem knew
she would die, even as her sandal-shod feet beat out a
death rhythm against the yacht's fiberglass shell.

No one else appeared from the gangway. The Colombian, ignoring the deep purple face of his choking companion, scrambled to his hands and knees and headed
for the stairway leading to the dock. Diem lost sight of
the congressman, his attention now fully on the rapidly
moving figure of his primary target. The man ignored
the steps, instead leaping from the deck and landing hard
on the dock more than ten feet below him. The Viet
almost pulled the trigger then, the man's face welling up
in the scope like a gas-filled balloon. It would have made
a nice shot, he thought.

Several seconds sped by as the Colombian gathered
his senses. The howl of sirens was a living thing as
emergency vehicles poured into the marina area, their
lights flashing as they bumped and ground their way
along the cluttered sidewalks, the streets bumper-to-
bumper with stalled traffic. The Colombian suddenly
leapt to his feet and began running for the open gate
leading from the dock out into the street. Vulnerability
was written all over the man's face as he dashed for the
safety of the assembled crowd. Diem could see it clearly,
could recognize the panic and determination to escape
the trap he knew had been sprung. The Viet had seen
the same look on many other faces just before he slammed
the gates of hell down on them with a single impulse to
his finger.

The Colombian reached the point Diem had selected
for him to die on. A slight adjustment of the barrel

brought the crossed lines inside the scope to bear on the man's head, tiny adjustments being made by the shooter as he took into account the forward movement of the target, the slightly hazy background, and a hundred other considerations that were acknowledged and then solved without conscious thought as the Viet's finger released the sear holding the firing pin at ready. A slight *pop* erupted from the rifle's muzzle as one hundred grains of copper-jacketed lead kicked up their heels and sped downrange. Diem maintained the scope on target, the weapon's recoil nonexistent due to the small caliber. His lips curled in contentment as a hole appeared without warning just below the Colombian's left eye, the orb itself flying out of its socket and onto the dock, where it would become a treat for a starving gull.

The Colombian's legs turned to rubber, his motor functions either totally blown out because of the bullet's damage to the core area of his brain, or disrupted enough so that he couldn't collect and distribute enough physical and mental information to save his life. Pawing at the slight, bleeding hole in his upper cheek, the man spun to the right, then collapsed on the dock, rolling several times before coming to a stop. His sudden blindness in one eye registered as an errant finger poked its way into the bloodied socket where his eye used to be. The dying man's roar of fear could be heard even above the shrill caterwaul of the ambulances as they arrived, shocking the crowd into silence as they watched one of their fellow beings fight for his life.

Diem automatically recocked the weapon, chambering his second round and adjusting the scope so he now had another power's worth of magnification at his disposal. The Colombian was nearly still now, his body bent at the waist and cocked at an angle which allowed the Viet a fairly clean shot into the side of the Latin's head. The sniper glued the butt of his weapon into the pocket of his shoulder, clutching the rear portion of the sling with his left hand so that the rifle was firmly locked into position. The second round was a special one, prepared by Diem that morning more for its visual effect than anything else. He'd learned the technique from an Australian SAS trooper who swore by his work, and Diem had enjoyed the opportunity to prove the man correct. Using his knife's keen edge the Viet had carefully cut the very tip of the bullet away, leaving a flat surface where once there had been a pronounced point. He'd then slowly cut a cross-notch into the round, the dual trenches fairly deep across the nose of the bullet, becoming shallower as they slipped down the round's sides. Upon impact this field-expedient "dum-dum" would break apart into four jagged sections, causing tremendous tissue and bone damage as it tumbled like a spastic gymnast through the target area.

With the scope's reticle once again locked in place, Diem took up trigger slack. The Colombian's head was rolling slightly to and fro, his tongue half-severed and hanging like a wet towel from between his cruel lips. Paramedics were beginning to move forward toward the dying figure lying crumpled on the blood-stained dock, their eyes sweeping up toward where the fire fighters were trying to get water on the furiously burning yacht's deck. An errant breeze blew the putrid smell of burning human flesh into Diem's wrinkled nose. The Vietnamese took it all in, letting off the shot even as several onlookers were overcome with the meaty smell and began vomiting on themselves as well as the sidewalk.

A paramedic pulled his hand back just as the bullet caught the Colombian behind the temple. The head col-

lapsed like a fermented melon, brain matter and blood
spilling as one onto the dock, soaking the emergency
technician's Nikes in a flood of busted bone, torn tissue,
and ruptured cells. All that was left intact was the lower
jaw and the nose, which had somehow combined so that
they formed a grotesque sculpture of stained ivory and
teak-colored flesh. The med-tec took one hard look at
the mass of mess at his gooey feet, then turned and ran
screaming back into the crowd.

Diem was already pulling the length of the rifle parallel
to his body. Clutching the weapon close into him, he
rolled quickly into the safety of the hotel room, letting
loose of the Ruger and grabbing a handful of blanket
material in the same motion. With a powerful tug he
jerked the makeshift shooting mat into the room with
him, swiftly finding the spent cartridge from the first shot
and pocketing it. Sliding the glass door shut, the Viet
rapidly broke the rifle down into its three primary com-
ponents, stuffing each into a hard leather suitcase made
especially for this purpose. Finished with his breakdown,
Diem scanned the room for anything missed during his
earlier clean-up, then scooted through the door linking
his to the Trung brothers' now-vacant room. Locking the
door behind him, the shooter lifted the bedside phone
and quickly punched in a 1–800 number. He gave a brisk
yet relaxed message to the person answering, then hung
up. It was time to move.

Diem opened the door leading into the hallway and
casually strolled down the rich carpeting, slipping into
the emergency exit stairwell just as one of the three
elevators serving the hotel reached his floor. The Viet
covered six flights of stairs in under two minutes, exiting
several floors below his original address. Smiling at a
Latin housekeeper whose towel truck was stacked with

the fruits of her labor, Diem made his way around the floor until he reached a room facing the opposite side of the city. Unlocking the door, he stepped inside, delighted to find all was as he'd left it the night before. Slipping the brown bag inside the closet, Diem called the front desk and asked for his messages. There was only one, a simple note saying that Uncle Ho was in town and anxious to see him that evening. The Trung brothers had made a clean escape!

The former Vietnamese sergeant switched on his color television and lay down on the king-sized bed facing it. His successful attack on the Colombian should be on the news any minute now, and he wanted to see how well the media would be able to exploit his gift. As an after-thought he once again picked up the phone and ordered a large meal from memory. All this work had made him hungry. A hamburger well-done arrived at his door just as the first footage of the conflagration outside his hotel began pouring across the 21-inch screen in living-dead color.

# CHAPTER

## 5

Thornton dropped the phone jack back on its cradle, indicating with a swift jerk of his thumb that it was time for him and Silver to join Bailey downstairs. The narc had made excellent connections, arriving in Los Angeles less than twenty-four hours after their initial conversation. They would be meeting in the Hyatt's lobby, having lunch out on the street-side terrace facing Sunset Boulevard.

Silver shrugged into a light sport coat, a faint bruise on his cheek bearing witness to the week's intensive training. Brushing his long, dark hair in the full length mirror of Bo's room, he admired himself for a moment, then turned to Thornton. "Heard from Linda lately?" he asked. Linda was Bo's girl, a handful of beauty, wit, and charm who had captured the big commando's heart with nary a shot fired in anger.

"She's still in Paris, ringing up a pretty penny on our

charge card from what she told me last night. Should be flying back from England in another week. At least that's the plan for now." Bo straightened his turtleneck, slipping into his own coat and feeling for the Crawford "Leopard" he'd picked up while attending a local knife show. The folder was state-of-the art, featuring a liner lock and 3½-inch blade ground from stainless steel. Brushed to an aircraft gray, the Leopard could be opened using one hand and was as silent as the ocean's depths while doing so. It was a flat, light, extremely sharp tool, which Thornton could appreciate for city wear.

"Frank should be in tonight. He's driving a rental up from San Diego as soon as he closes shop. If you decide we're gonna party with Calvin on this gig, we'll need at least two more hands. Any ideas?"

Thornton shook his head at the former ranger who was his neighbor and best friend. Just as Jason was concerned about their manning roster, so was Bo. Dave Lee, the only active-duty member of SPRINGBLADE, was still recovering from the multiple wounds and cuts he'd taken while hunting down Angel Barahone in Nicaraqua. Thornton was also concerned that Lee might be getting a little gun-shy about going over the wire with the team. He'd been the only one to take major hits on at least two missions now, and was joking with Thornton about ". . . being a bullet sponge for you assholes!" after being med-evaced down to Panama once General Gaston had extracted the two-man team from the border. The truth was Thornton never expected his charter to extend past the original contract offered by Conrad Billings. They were now entering their fifth mission as a covert arm of the Bush Administration, and manpower was becoming critical. "I'd like to bring the Russian along, but he's still in debrief. Chuikov would be a strong addition, and he needs the work.''

Silver nodded in agreement. They'd pulled the SPETS-NAZ colonel's nuts out of the fire on their last outing, and Jason had come to know the big Russian as both a friend and fighter. ''Bannion?''

''I wish. Mike's hip-deep in DEA SLAM operations in Burma. He's got his own team now, and although I know he'd like to come, he wouldn't leave his people if they're operational.''

Jason opened the door to the room and both men stepped into the deserted hallway. The Hyatt was not an ornate hotel, but it was extremely comfortable and tastefully decorated. Upon reaching the elevator Silver popped the clear plastic down button. ''Maybe our man Calvin can provide some horsepower,'' he offered. ''After all, he found Mike for us and that worked out fine.''

Thornton grunted. He himself possessed a tidy little list of retired special ops personnel from which he could draw. Of course, Frank Hartung could pull names and addresses from his head if they needed to do some creative recruiting. Hartung, also retired from the Forces, was Thornton's business partner in a dive shop called Heavy Hook. If there was some credible talent out there Frank would know about it.

The double doors opened, revealing a crowd of tourists all speaking German. The two shadow warriors politely pushed their way free of the throng, hanging a left and walking through the wide doorway leading into the hotel's eating area. A petite Salvadoran waitress flashed them a delicate smile, her brown eyes deep and inviting. Silver mentioned their reservation and she ushered them outside to where Bailey was already sitting. The sound of mid afternoon L.A. traffic greeted them, although it was strangely muted by the stucco wall separating the elevated patio from the sidewalk. As they approached the table, Thornton nudged Silver from behind. "Who the hell is that with Cal?" he whispered.

"The fuck if I know, maybe an intell specialist or something?" responded Jason.

"I *hate* surprises," moaned Bo inwardly as both men rose to greet them. Another new face in the ever-growing circle of faces that was slowly forming itself around Thornton's team. Soon they'd be on the "Today" show being interviewed by Bryant Gumball.

"Bo, Jason. Good to see you again!" said Bailey in greeting as he wrung their hands. Turning to his guest, he quickly introduced the man, and another round of handshakes and kind words were exchanged before the foursome sat down.

Bo studied the newcomer as Jason and Bailey began bantering about L.A. women. He was oriental, perhaps Chinese-American by the manner of his speech and dress. At roughly five-foot-eleven Thornton figured him to tip the scales just over 220 pounds, all of it apparently muscle. His hair was a rich black, worn very short and in combination with a Fu Manchu–style mustache. The eyes were piercing, and brown like Bo's. His smile was fast yet sincere, well modulated and precise in its inflections. Bo noted the Rolex GMT on the man's left wrist, an intricate gold ring bearing the Special Forces crest wrapped around the right ring finger. He figured their guest to be in his late forties even though he moved and was built like someone ten years younger. Thornton decided he could like the man, who's name had been given as Alan Rowe.

"Who were you with?"

Rowe's attention shifted from Silver and Bailey to Bo, who was sipping at a cup of particularly good coffee. "The First, back in the late fifties. Ran sterile recon out of Thailand, all Asian teams, mostly border stuff. After that I went on loan to several cosponsored projects which Calvin would have to clear before I could talk about them, then hung it up to do other things of a tamer nature."

Thornton paused for a moment. He'd heard about the teams Rowe mentioned during his first tour in Vietnam. All Asian, very low profile. They'd walked all over the borders of China, Vietnam, Laos, you name it. Serious balls kind of guys whom you didn't run into very much. Alan was the first for Bo, who'd been around the SF community forever it seemed. "So you quit?"

Alan laughed, his face lighting up in a mass of crinkles and glimmers that brought a smile to everyone seated around the table. "No," replied Rowe once he'd simmered down. "I didn't 'quit,' just made a lateral transfer you might say. It's impossible to get out of SF if you love it as much as I do."

The waiter arrived to take their orders, and after he'd left, Bailey began talking. The morning's traffic and the isolation of the men's table in the corner of the patio made it as good a place as any for the DEA man to lay his cards on the table. "First off, Alan came at my request because I know the team's short on manpower. He was recommended to me by some folks who prefer not to do more than wish you well, but it's Bo's decision whether he straphangs or not.

"Besides possessing an S.O. background, Rowe here is an expert on the Vietnamese . . ."

"Alive or dead?" joked Silver. A polite ripple of laughter made its way around the table.

"Both," retorted Alan. "I made them a special project of my own when we began sending the troops in."

Bailey paused a moment, letting Rowe's point be made, then continued. "We've got a major problem taking place along our southern border which involves a shitpot of people, millions of dollars, and uncounted innocent lives. I've brought a full S-2 packet on the mission for each member of the team should you launch.

"In short, though, one former General Duc Phong has been building a paramilitary community of refugee Vietnamese out in Taos, New Mexico, for several years now. Phong has cultivated an intense loyalty among his people, many of whom are former ARVN soldiers. He's also built a very impressive network back into Southeast Asia among the drug lords, who we believe are providing hard intelligence about major shipments going to Phong's competition, the Latin cartels.

"Over the last six months, various agencies involved with border watch activities down Mexico way have been stumbling onto body dumps stretching across the whole lower half of the country. Primarily they center along the drug smuggling routes coming into Texas, Arizona, New Mexico, and now we're even finding bones and bullet casings in Southern California. Our own sources in the Vietnamese communities, the vast majority of which abhor Phong's criminal activities I would add, paint a picture of coordinated military-style operations aimed at ripping off the Latin smugglers for the financial benefit of their Viet counterparts."

Breakfast arrived, their meeting continuing as the men ate. "Phong is a familiar name. Where have I head it before?" asked Silver.

"Golden Tiger division commander. Balls made from stainless steel and a heart like a lion's. He was despised by many of his peers because he made them look bad in the field . . . meaning he actually fought the war," replied Thornton between bites.

Rowe agreed. "Phong got out of Vietnam just hours before the country fell. He came to America, settled in New Mexico, and tried to become an upstanding citizen. Things have been tough for the Vietnamese coming here. They are having to become a part of a culture totally unlike their own. They are facing discrimination when it used to be them against the 'lesser' races in their own country. Our own problems in dealing with the war haven't helped them, and so it goes.

"What the general is doing is basically what he understands is the only way for him and his people to survive comfortably in their new surroundings. Duc Phong was fairly clean during the war from what we know, but he understood how to play the game nonetheless. I believe, from studying this situation for several months, that Phong has hatched a plan to establish a criminal Vietnamese cartel here in the United States, funding it by ripping off the Mexicans, Colombians, Bolivians, and anyone else involved with them."

"You mean he's getting tipped as to what's coming across the border and hitting these caravans for all they're worth? He's gotta be crazy!" exclaimed Jason.

"Not really," offered Calvin. "Or at least not any crazier than the rest of them.

"Ever since King George let loose the dogs, the Latins have been working overtime to reestablish their trade centers. Our side's been scarfing up huge stockpiles of coke, hash, heroin, all that good shit. It's hurt the hell out of the boys Down South, and they're sincerely pissed at the recent profit margins.

"What they've done is start putting together heavily

armed bands of smugglers who ride shotgun on loads like we've never seen before. They use mule trains, each animal carrying from between 250 to 350 pounds of dope. You can't believe the routes they travel, real hells-on-earth affairs that are near impossible for us to find let alone set up interdiction efforts over. What kingpins like Canales, Noriega, Canos, and the others want is a series of massive distribution centers throughout the United States their organizations can draw off of . . .''

''A regular 'Dope-4-Less' chain of stores, huh?''

''That's right, Jason,'' continued Bailey. ''In addition it's meant to shove our efforts up our collective noses. They want us to know we can't stop them, that they can pour more in than we can out. The problem is they're right. We've only got so many men and women, so much money, and so much room to operate. The flaming liberal interpretation of our own system of laws is creating a void for these assholes to strangle us at will in. Their lawyers talk while the client walks. Meanwhile Mr. Average Joe America buries his son, or daughter, or wife because they couldn't 'just say no.' ''

The group was silent for several minutes after Bailey finished speaking. Their waiter returned to clear the table, bringing coffee as the second half of the meeting began. A long, tall blonde in ass-tight leather pants and an open white blouse strode by on the sidewalk, her eyes hidden behind expensive sunglasses. They all watched in appreciation.

''I'm in lust,'' murmured Rowe. ''Be easy to do a hundred push-ups over that.'' His companions agreed.

''So,'' exclaimed Thornton, ''where the hell were we before our dicks got hard?'' Laughter greeted his sage observation.

Bailey picked up the beat. ''What we've got is a regular range war going on. Phong's assholes are pushing Latin-bought dope they've ripped off into a brand new distribution system which will take years for us to get people into.

"The Latins on the other hand are gearing up for one big confrontation with Phong because they're not going to lose what they've worked so hard to get. We know a contract was recently let out by a major figure in Colombia with the general's name on it. How that's gonna go down back at the ranch we can only guess.

"Then there's the casualty rate on our side . . ."

At this they all leaned forward, their coffee forgotten. The waiter, halfway to their table, decided these gringos didn't want a refill and quickly found someone else to occupy his time.

"Our reserve team, is that what you're talking about?" asked Thornton, his voice low and sincere in a slightly dangerous sort of way.

"Roger that, Bo. That team first appeared to have vanished into the desert. We never found shit, nothing. Then this last caravan dump turns up the team leader's beret. You guys didn't know these boys, I've checked already. They were a hardcore team of citizen-soldiers just trying to carry out a mission that, in my professional opinion, wasn't explained too clearly to them.

"From the history we dug up on the dude found with the hat, it's more than likely they got surprised by a load coming through and waxed. There's been others, mostly Border Patrol types and some DEA. Lots of hick town officers who were out wandering their necks of the woods and never came back. I'm telling you straight out there's a full-blown war taking place on *our* side of the border and the public isn't even half-aware of it."

"So call Dan-fucking-Rather and let him open the eyes

and minds of America!'' scoffed Jason. ''And what about our favorite president? Why doesn't he blow the whistle on this?''

Rowe intervened. ''Politics. Mexico is so fucked up that we could release a shit-storm if we open this up. You know the deal in Central America, El Salvador is once again looking bad, Nicaragua's a wild card, Honduras and Costa Rica are straddling the fence, and Panama is setting itself up to become our fifty-first state.

''In Southeast Asia we're *finally* opening up all the networks and connections we enjoyed during Vietnam. At the same time we've got the heavy-metal drug connections there to contend with and there's a balance to be maintained. Contrary to popular misconception the rest of the world isn't the least bit interested in how America feels about certain issues. Besides the fact we don't share cultural ties, there's the reality that Uncle Sam has fucked a lot of folks around the globe these last two hundred and some odd years. We tend to forget that; they don't.''

Thornton interjected. ''Okay. We know we're not going to solve this sad old world's problems sitting here on Sunset. Sounds to me like Conrad wants Phong taken down. I have no problem with that. But . . . and this is a big but . . . I want the option of whacking the character who paid for the Berets getting hit. King George gives us that and we'll fly.''

Bailey grunted. ''The dude you're talking about is our Mr. Canales from Mexico. If the bastard comes over the border, he's open season for the team. If not . . .''

''No sweat, squid. We'll figure a way to get the pig on the other side of his sty; I'll leave that to the sergeant major. He's suckered the best of them into a three-ring kill zone, as we all well know.''

Their laughter at the reference to Frank Hartung's devious mind broke the tension that had set in. Bailey ordered more coffee, which was poured rapidly as the waiter sensed these were men whose business he didn't want to know anything about. When he had scampered off to the kitchen, the conversation resumed.

"Is Alan here to go operational?" asked Bo.

"If you feel good about him, yes. His background is solid or he wouldn't be here. His expertise on the Viets will be an added plus for you, and he's hell on wheels with just about every light and heavy weapon known to man."

Thornton turned to Silver, who nodded. Focusing his attention on Rowe, Bo asked the man if he wanted to join the team. Alan Rowe gave one of his best smiles in response, he and Bo shaking hands. "Welcome back on active duty, Sarge. You're gonna earn your pay on this one, but Calvin's pockets are deep. Aren't they, boy?"

Bailey grimaced at the mention of money. It was he who had to broach the question of finances to his boss, Conrad Billings. All of SPRINGBLADE's "black" funds came from dope money captured in the war on drugs. There were no taxes levied on the team for their earnings, and no records kept. That was part of the deal. These men had lived and fought for the country, been wounded in its wars, and brought home their own. Bo Thornton believed in his country's economic concept, and he wanted himself as well as his men to share in its fruits. They earned their fees the old-fashioned way, through sweat, blood, and rock-hard determination to succeed. Damn right they got paid, just like everybody else. "How much?" asked the former SEAL.

"I'll let you know," smirked Bo. "But I can say it'll be more than we've gotten to date, and I want Lee and

Bannion paid as if they were along for the ride."

"Shit!" Bailey looked worried. The men who were his friends laughed at the young narc's discomfort. Being a bean counter wasn't his cup of tea.

Rowe pushed away from the table. "If you'll excuse me, I need to run upstairs and use the little boy's room." The chatter dropped back into talk about women, guns, and extremely fast cars as the newest addition to the SPRINGBLADE team headed for the elevator.

After several seconds the huge double doors slid open, but before Alan could step in, he was pushed aside by a heavy set thug with wildly frizzed hair. "Outta way, pal! Comin' through ya!" Behind the body builder strode a thin young man dressed in black satin. His hair was long, his eyes hidden from view behind mirrored glasses. Both stormed into the elevator's tiny room, the thug punching the CLOSE button just as Rowe stepped in behind them.

"We're priority, Marvin. Punch in the key and let the Jap here catch his floor on the ride down," ordered the skinny geek. Marvin grinned at Alan, pushing into the slot a key that, when turned, would take the elevator directly to the penthouse. Alan moved to punch in his own floor, but a solid fist wrapped around the former trail runner's wrist before his finger could hit the button.

"Din't you hear Mr. Grind, asshole? You wait until we're off, *then* you can go to your shithole room!"

Behind him, Alan heard the creep now known as "Grind" giggle. "Easy, Marv, this dude probably don't know he's on an elevator with the world's greatest rock guitarist. We got a heavy gig tonight, dude. I need my axe for a jam and ain't got but five to get it before the limo's gotta get back to the stage, you dig?"

His wrist still encased in the bodyguard's hand, Rowe turned and faced Grind. "No, asshole, I don't 'dig' what you're saying at all. In fact, I don't give a fat rat's ass about your gig, your axe, or this stupid toad's face. I suggest you order Mr. Brain Matter to let loose of me or I'll be forced to defend myself."

Grind's face turned beet red. The rock musician, followed the world over by his fans and drug dealers, exploded. No one talked to "The Grind" like this! Punching the STOP button with his bony fist, the near-frantic guitarist brought the elevator to a sudden halt between floors. Glaring at the Oriental in front of him, he suddenly slapped Rowe across the face. Stepping back in satisfaction he ordered the hulking bruiser who was his personal hatchet man to finish the job. "We'll leave the legal stuff to the lawyers, Marv. In the meantime, kick this dickhead's ass!"

Marvin grinned, then dropped his lower jaw in surprise as Alan deftly twisted then slid his captured wrist free of the ape's iron grasp. "Here's a little tune I wrote myself," he told the two men. "It's called 'I Got My Ass Kicked by a Dickhead,' and I hope you like it!"

Marvin recovered from his shock and threw a wide right at Rowe's head. Alan sidestepped the punch, popping Grind in the throat with a sharp chop that froze the singer's vocal cords so he was unable to utter a sound. As the musician's hands flew up to cover his suddenly silent big mouth, Rowe dropped into a low crouch that avoided a second punch, this time a left hook, from Marvin. As the blow whistled harmlessly over his head only to connect with Grind's jaw behind him, Alan pushed upward using all the power he could muster from his thick calves and thighs. His right hand formed into a steel-like knife's blade, the "retired" Special Forces sergeant rammed the wicked edge of flesh hard up between Marvin's legs. Without stopping, he then aimed a vicious chop at the man's exposed neck, dropping him to the elevator's floor in a pool of warm vomit.

Spinning in the narrow confines of the cubicle, Alan grabbed the stunned rocker by his hair and pulled him upright. Nose to nose, Rowe took in the fear plastered across the suddenly defenseless guitarist's face. It made him feel good. "Okay, dipwad, here's the story. You've fucked with the wrong dude, and you've lost. By the way, I'm Chinese, not Japanese. But I understand your mistake 'cause all you white punks look the same to me, too.

"I've got a hunch you've been putting dog-breath here on folks who've crossed your path for some time now. You're nothing but an overpaid jerkoff who's used to getting his own way. Well, I'm not fucking impressed!

"So, what I'm going to do is teach you a lesson. You won't learn anything from it because you're too stupid. But it will make me feel better and may save some poor son-of-a-bitch a beating from one of your goons in the future."

Hearing Rowe's words, the frightened guitarist attempted to break away from Alan's grip on him. After a few seconds he knew it was futile, and tears began welling up in his glazed-over eyes. Rowe knew he had to move fast before hotel security started checking into the stalled elevator.

"You fuck with me, and I'll let loose some friends of mine who are experts in tax audits, private investigation, investigative journalism, et cetera. I can put your skinny ass back behind the counter at McDonald's, son. Do you believe me?"

The rocker nodded, a foul smell coming up from his

pants as he dumped a load in them out of sheer fear. Without warning, Alan grabbed the young man's right hand and popped each finger out of its joint. As the rock musician struggled in new found pain, Rowe did the same to his other hand, taking care to fracture its thumb and index finger so the boy wouldn't be able to pick more than his nose for about six months. Behind him, on the floor, Marvin was stirring. Rowe punched the release button and felt the elevator moving upward to the penthouse. When it arrived he turned to the guitar player, who was now curled up on the vomit-soaked carpet of the lift next to his hired hand. "Remember my words, Mr. Grind. You have no idea who I am, but I feel quite close to you. Have a good day, and enjoy the 'gig' tonight."

Punching the STOP button one more time, Alan ripped the key from its sheath and pocketed it. He would dump the tiny piece of metal somewhere along his route back down the emergency stairs. Now the elevator was frozen where it was, with neither of the two men capable of doing much more than some slow crawling. Hurrying to the marked exit door, he rapidly moved back down to the floor above his own, stepping into the hallway and striding around the floor to the second set of stairs. Once safe in his room, Rowe phoned the front desk and asked for Bailey. When the narc stopped laughing at Alan's recounting of his "fight" with the music crowd, he told the newest SPRINGBLADER they'd be up in a few moments. "Just lay low, Al. I doubt we'll hear anything from this clown, but there's no sense tempting fate."

Alan agreed. "You don't think Thornton will be pissed at me, do you? I mean, I just shot my wad about what a pro I am and two seconds later I'm kicking the shit outta some long-haired pill popper."

Calvin laughed. "Hey, don't sweat it. When we get some free time remind me to tell you about a would-be mugger in D.C. who 'met' Bo under similar circumstances. At least your boy will be able to sit down!"

Hanging up, Alan glanced at his reflection in the mirror. Now what the hell did Bailey mean by that?

# CHAPTER
# 6

Bailey finished nodding, the phone tucked up under his chin as he scribbled notes on a pad provided by a secretary who looked as if she'd been recruited from Hell itself. Around the office, Thornton and team were killing time, waiting for final preparations and commitments to be issued from Washington. Frank Hartung had gotten in the night before, rooming with Alan at another hotel down the street. After the encounter with "Fingers" Grinder, as he was now affectionately known, Calvin had decided to split the team until they launched.

"Yeah, got it all. No shit? No doubts in my mind who hit the pukeball. Nawww, we're looking good at this end. Yeah, yeah, I'll get back with you tonight. Bye!" The young narc replaced the phone and signaled to the group to follow him into one of the large soundproofed meeting chambers the L.A. DEA people used for mission planning sessions. As one, they stood, exchanging wisecracks and finally trooping after the gung-ho agent's retreating figure.

Bailey gestured they should each grab a well-worn chair. The evil office worker who'd slammed a yellow note pad down on Calvin's borrowed desk had done the same for the rest of the team, providing two sharpened pencils and a pot of coffee with cups as well. Everybody got comfortable as Bailey began speaking.

"Here's what Billings has for us. Bo gets his budget approved although Conrad did a double-dump when he heard the terms and figure." Calvin smiled as he watched a huge grin crease the big man's face. Thornton had demanded nearly ten thousand more per man than their last outing, with a full twenty-five thousand more for himself. In addition, both Lee and Bannion would be paid as if they were along for the ride, Thornton's feeling being that they would have been except for Dave's wounds and Mike's priority duty with SLAM. Rowe came in at the new wage and compensation package, the money going to an account in Europe. Bo had known the money was there, just as he knew the government's accountants would do all they could to hoard the funds as if the money were their own.

Allowing the high-fives and handshakes to subside, Bailey continued. "We'll isolate here in L.A., launching into New Mexico within forty-eight hours. You all saw the evening news, but if not, one of our asshole major Colombian dirtbags went and got himself severely whacked in Florida yesterday. Our people on the scene are calling it a military hit, complete with LAW rockets and one very accomplished marksman with a taste for visual effects. There are no leads, no witnesses, but one very hard suspect's name is being mentioned . . ."

"General Duc Phong?" offered Rowe.

"Give the FNG a cheap cigar," responded Bailey. "Our boy just took care of canceling his contract as well as the Colombian's, plus there's a major political scandal brewing because some dipshit congressman was found stumbling around the docks with a load of coke in his swim trunks!" Another burst of laughter shook the group, everyone of them having seen the all too self-serving side of those who craved the attention a soapbox offered.

Thornton spoke up, his coffee cup already half-empty as he washed a slightly stale hunk of coffee cake down. "We need to get in touch with someone having first-hand information about Phong. Does Billings have that kind of hook?"

"Negative," replied Calvin. "The general runs a tight company when it comes to security. There's leaks, sure. But finding someone *we* can trust to give us some good poop is a different story."

Hartung let loose with a loud belch, bringing the entire discussion to a momentary stop. Having everyone's attention, the retired sergeant major lit a massive stogie. "We know this Phong asshole was a big-shot general in the ARVN, and we know he had strong ties to the little people in the provisionals. I got some old running mates in the Vietnamese communities who owe old Frank a favor or two. Give me a phone and an office, I'll get the network cooking and see what we come up with."

Thornton nodded in agreement. Frank's "network" was one of the best in the business. The old warrior's reputation was 22k in special ops circles, and he delighted in keeping up with what was *really* going down around the world. If there was a way to burrow into Duc Phong's scheme, Frank would be their best bet at finding it ASAP.

"You got it, Frank! I'll get the warthog in the outer

office to find some digs for you once we break up. Bo? You want Jason and me to start scouting equipment?" Bailey turned an inquiring eye to the One-Zero, taking a deep drag off his cigarette while waiting for Bo to answer.

"No. You and I need to get together and do some pre-mission shit. I need access to the DEA's files in New Mexico, and you'll have to punch that up for me. Alan and Jason can start assembling a war chest for us, keeping in mind we'll be operating in the desert. We'll pull the serious weaponry from the SEALs in Diego, although the nuts-and-bolts items can be bought off the shelf here."

Rowe lifted a hand. "Does this mean we're going to hit Phong in Taos?"

Thornton shook his head. "Negative. That would be easier, but the attention would blow this whole op to hell and back. Nope, we've got to lock in on something which will pull the general into the field with his troops. It needs to be a sweet pot, but somewhere isolated. If we can get Canales in on the deal, that would solve two problems. Right now all I can tell you is I want to draw our Vietnamese snake out into the open so we can cut off his head with as little commotion as possible."

Jason agreed. "Al and I need to get moving if we're launching as soon as Cal says. I'll need some 'gimme the shit now' passes for both Rowe and me, not to mention a sturdy van for transport. We gonna keep our rooms at the hotels?"

"Roger that," replied Bailey. "We'll do all our planning here, but the rooms are fine as they are. Keep your gear semipacked in case we get the green light sooner than expected. Watch the girls; they're nice to pet, but remember, these are L.A. ladies. They listen and learn, and they know how to use information where it'll do them the most good. Keep the booze to a minimum, and make sure you've got my beeper number in case you need to call.''

Everyone jotted down the narc's mobile answering service number while Bailey lit another smoke.

''If that's it, I gotta get going on these calls,'' said Hartung. ''There's bound to be a few PRU vets in the AO, maybe the general is working that end of it. Be a big help to him to have a cadre of seasoned recon studs around. He'd have to recruit and that means talking to people.''

Thornton agreed. ''Go for it, Frank. In the meantime I'll pull what I can from the DEA's computers here, then start working on breaking out some hard intelligence on what might be in the works coming over from Southeast Asia. Maybe Mike's folks in Burma can open that door?''

Bailey shrugged. ''SLAM shit is pretty hush-hush, even for us. The risk of compromise and its reward is so great . . . well, those boys spell OPSEC in blood if you get my drift. We can try, though, with Mike there, it might help.''

The meeting at a close, they grabbed whatever they'd brought with them and headed for the door. Calvin stopped Frank, and together they slipped down a side hall. Thornton stood off by himself going over the rest of the afternoon in his mind. Jason, knowing his friend expected them to get on with their end of things, tugged at Rowe's sports jacket. ''Let's get going, Al. Bo's got a ton of shit to think about, plus he'll be off and running once Calvin unloads the sergeant major on some poor office pogue.''

Rowe smiled and nodded, knowing what the team's

demo specialist said was true. "You guys always get short-notice gigs like this?" he asked.

Jason laughed. "Yeah, Cal has a habit of dropping these little gems on us just before the clock strikes midnight. I haven't been on one as quick coming off the line as this one, but if Bo feels we can tie a knot in it, well, he's the boss."

Alan shrugged. His own call from the agent's office in D.C. had put him on the next thing smoking out to Los Angeles. Rowe was used to funny calls from funny people. He'd remained involved with the direct action side of the house since leaving the service formally. His business back home would be fine while he was away, two lovely daughters and a strong son watching over it. Alan's wife had gone back to China, the strangeness of America too much for the woman. Rowe didn't hold it against her, in fact he admired her will to make such a bold decision. In the meantime he'd continued doing those things he enjoyed and felt were worthwhile, believing that in the end the satisfaction of a life well lived would be a fitting epitaph.

The elevator doors slid open, and the two men stepped inside, each lost in his own thoughts and world.

# CHAPTER
**———**
# 7

They were gathered around a long, oval desk with no sides or drawers, which had been hand-rubbed to a high gloss by its maker over one hundred years before. The desk had been in Phong's family ever since, and he continued its care according to the instructions given by the original craftsman to Phong's ancestors. The general himself was center stage, his face serious as he leaned on both hands over a large map carefully laid on in front of him. Assembled around the oval platform were Phong's advisors and officers, each quietly offering his own version of how the plan might best succeed. Everyone was standing, as there were no chairs present; this was a working session.

The Vietnamese had been highly pleased with the results of Diem's excursion to Florida. He'd watched every major network's report of the Colombian's death several times over, relishing the enormous amount of imagination and skill Diem had used to announce to the world what Phong wanted said. One tourist had been fortunate enough to be filming the startled bastard as he attempted to run to safety, capturing the very moment the sergeant's bullet sucker-punched him in the face. Phong ordered a video made for his private viewing.

Reports from the general's friends told of mass shock and confusion within the ranks of the Southern cartels. Naturally the rest of the idiots were throwing up walls of steel around themselves, a wasted effort as Diem and the Trung brothers were en route home. The word was definitely out, according to the general's cohorts and associates, the brightness of the burning yacht and the cracked open shell of the Colombian's head testimony to the power of Phu Dung.

One report had troubled the general, though. It had come from one of his border agents, an old Indian whom he paid to listen as he bartered cheap artifacts in the tourist town facing Old Mexico. Canales, of all his enemies, was responding to the assassination of his amigo in a manner completely unexpected by Phu Dung's leader. The head of the closest and most powerful Mexican smuggling family had called a council of war, dispatching a flying column of gunmen to a desert airstrip from where, according to the Indian, they would launch a heavy strike against General Phong. Canales apparently was not content to sit and wring his hands at the sudden turn of events. Luckily his men talked too much when they were in town gathering supplies.

The map they were studying was of the area containing the airstrip. It was one used by smugglers of all sorts, an empty stretch of hard-packed sand with several blackened 55-gallon drums lying on their sides to be used as ground beacons for the pilots. The flight patterns taken by the airborne pirates were dangerous in themselves. All required flying less than fifty feet off the ground, twisting and turning through dark canyons and over broad expanses of barren desert. Many of the planes carried expensive radar systems, sensors and displays that gave the pilot an exact picture of his surroundings. Those who chose not to invest in the sophisticated electronics so necessary for today's smuggling efforts were either caught by National Guard aircraft or were lost to accidents. Every so often a burned-out hulk would be spotted and reported to Phong, testimony to the risks they were all taking.

As the Viet traced a nicotine-stained fingertip along a proposed route of travel, one of his advisors was speaking. The man was one of the many who had served with the general during the war and had joined him to escape the living death that was civilian life in America. "We can muster perhaps fifty fighters. Their transportation will be somewhat of a problem but nothing we cannot overcome. The Indian believes the strip is held by an advance party, maybe ten men. The others are due in within twenty-four hours by air. From there they will move against us, although how we do not know at this time."

Phong nodded, standing upright and stretching away the slight cramp that was developing in his lower back from bending over. Age, he thought. Once I could develop a campaign and sleep only two hours a day. Now my muscles deceive me and my eyes ache to be closed. No general can defeat the enemy we call age. Turning to the man, Phong waved his hand, a gesture meaning the man should hold his tongue. When Phong spoke, it was with the voice of a man coached in the use of what military men called a "command voice." It gathered everyone there in, lending them courage and will, giving an order they knew must be carried out. Duc Phong had been born to be a general, and he well knew it. "Phu Dung cannot spare fifty of our best soldiers to handle this incursion. Send twenty-five with heavy weapons, using the helicopters to put them in place before the arrival of the others.

"Our own organization has used this strip many times. I want the pilots to fly directly in and unload the assault force so they can engage Canales's security element immediately. Half of them will flee anyhow; the desert will swallow their flesh and bleach their bones within days. Have the force commander allow our enemies to land, then wipe them out before they can set foot on the ground. Burn the aircraft, leave the bodies where they lie. Oh, have the men plant these fools' heads as a warning to Canales and his band of whores. We've no more time for these stupid games of his. Any questions?"

For the next fifteen minutes his staff hammered out the final points of the airlift and ambush. It would require moving many men and pieces of equipment quickly and secretly. This they could do. The raiding party's commander was selected and approved by Phong, who then left the details to his planners. Now he could only wait. One challenge had already been smashed, and now another was rising in its place. Like the phoenix, he thought as he headed for the sauna and a brace of nubile twins he'd flown in from Houston for some relaxation. Like Phu Dung itself his enemies were being reborn. Strange how fate plays with us, he ventured to himself. Opening the door to the softly lit spa, he was greeted with the sight of two lovely young women standing nude before the bubbling pool.

It promised to be a long night.

# CHAPTER

**████████**

## 8

The single Blackhawk came in low, its heavy rotors whipping the machine through the hot desert air in a frenzy of noise and movement. Inside the troop carrier, Thornton sat up near the pilot's compartment. His face was hidden, encircled as it was by the lightweight pilot's helmet he'd accepted from the crew chief before takeoff. The big commando wore a fresh set of U.S.-issue desert camouflage, its tans, blacks, and whites forming a pattern based on months of study by the Army. It was an excellent uniform—if you were fighting an enemy in Arizona or New Mexico, where it had been developed. Bo had heard that once the uniform began being used in the Middle East, it became apparent the research and development team should have done their homework there. Deserts, like people, are different in their makeup and personality.

Thornton liked the uniform anyhow.

The rest of the team was scrunched up in the belly of the metal bird, their bodies wrapped in the same soft material as their One-Zero's. Fully rigged combat harnesses hung from their shoulders and were cinched around their waists. Each had a desert-pattern boonie hat shoved down the front of his fatigue shirt, the newness of the hats already being erased as the men twisted, folded, and crunched the headgear to suit their own tastes. Silver and Rowe had pushed hard enough to get the team's favorite weapon, the CAR-15 or Colt Commando, issued en masse by SEAL TEAM ONE. They'd drawn Glock 17s as well, with ten magazines per carbine and three per pistol part of the deal. Each man was issued two M26 fragmentation grenades, as well as one claymore. It was necessarily light armament, as they would be conducting a POW snatch and would need to be able to move quickly. The CARs and Glocks gave the team an enormous firepower advantage, plus there would be an extraction ship with escort standing by when they needed support.

As usual each SPRINGBLADER was carrying a knife of some sort. Despite the amount of technology available, the feeling that came from having a good piece of sharpened steel at his side couldn't be done away with. Thornton had ensured that each of his people was well versed in the skill of combat bladesmanship, an art far different from the more structured approaches taken by "professional" knife fighters. Bo and his team had taken the game to the hilt on more than one occasion. They were seasoned, blooded, and respectful of the power a good knife possessed in the right hands.

Jason had swung by and asked Hartsfield to throw in one of his handy *kozukas*, the battle *khukuri* already sheathed and razor sharp. The massive knife was strapped securely to Silver's harness, the wrapped handle tilted slightly forward so Jason could lever it out in an instant. Phill had sharpened the back of Silver's knife so that, unlike the traditional *khukuri*, it had two cutting planes, a feature that would allow the compact ranger the added advantage of a serious backstroke during close combat. The *kozuka* was an ancient Japanese utility knife, meant for everyday chores such as cutting and slicing. It rode neatly in a pouch built into the *khukuri*'s sheath, a finger's pull away from action. Hartung, on the other hand, had strapped his AMK SERE onto the right shoulder strap of his battle gear. Its micarta handle rode upside down, the sheath allowing this mode of carry due to its custom construction by a saddle maker Bo knew in Cannon Beach. The sergeant major was the only team member not carrying a Glock, which he humorously referred to as a piece of "tactical Tupperware" because of its polymer construction. Frank's side arm of choice continued to be a Browning Hi-Power, which he'd been able to bring up with him from Heavy Hook.

Both Thornton and Rowe had elected to carry the new Applegate Combat Smatchet from Buck Knives. They'd stumbled upon the updated version of the historic old weapon while wandering around Hollywood one evening after dinner. The smatchet was originally influenced by the Welsh *cledd*, an early Celtic sword that used a broad leaf pattern as its blade format. Applegate had decided to update the World War II version of the knife, putting it into production in a limited run of five hundred pieces. The new improved smatchet offered its owner a full 10½ inches of double-edged stainless steel, a Lexan handle molded to the full tang, and a practical Cordura sheath. Both men had recognized the overwhelming tactical advantage such a knife had, a tribute to Applegate's un-

derstanding of knife combatives, which the renowned
former OSS colonel had earned up close and firsthand.

Calvin Bailey sat next to Bo, his own battle harness
set up much the way he'd worn it with the SEALs. Bailey
would be straphanging the mission, coming along to ob-
serve and lend a helping hand if needed. Bailey preferred
to carry two distinctly different edged weapons, one
which Hartung had drooled over when he'd seen it at the
DEA launch site outside of Taos. Slung from his right
side so it rode low along his hip was an exact replica of
Peter LaGana's "Vietnam Fighting Tomahawk." La-
Gana had formed the American Tomahawk Company in
the midsixties, making his fame by supplying U.S. ser-
vicemen with a lightweight, hand-forged tactical 'hawk,
which was then painted olive-drab. The tomahawk caught
on, ending up on the belts of a variety of special forces
types and recon people. It was rumored more than a few
VC heads were "liberated" by Mr. LaGana's handy tool,
much to the embarrassment of certain commanders, who
outlawed the 'hawks soon after. Strapped up high on his
left shoulder was a custom-made fighter from Jimmy
Lile. "The Death Wind" was sleek, light, and terribly
sharp, made only for opening up unprotected bellies or
draining gaping throats of their life's juices. Together
both weapons made Bailey an arsenal of edged mayhem
should the situation require it.

The copilot turned, tapping Bo on the shoulder with
a gloved hand. Holding up five fingers, he indicated they
would be setting the team down within minutes. Thornton
nodded, jabbing Bailey and passing the signal on. Within
thirty seconds the team was wide awake, carefully pulling
back on their carbines' charging handles, then checking
to make sure safeties were on. The crew chief slid first
one, then the other cabin door open so a hot rush of dry

desert air suddenly flooded the cramped compartment. Hartung had scrounged up a set of tanker's goggles for each man, and everyone nodded to each other and gave a hearty thumbs-up to the veteran noncom as bits of sand and debris bounced harmlessly off their clear plastic lenses.

It had been Frank's rapid phone work that had brought the news of Phong's intended raid to their attention. He'd first contacted an old friend in the Special Operations Association, who in turn had given him the number of the Vietnamese Rangers Association. Their membership was made up of men who'd served as Rangers, or with the Vietnamese Rangers as advisors during the war. Two phone calls later and Hartung was talking with a man who enjoyed close ties with a small, close-knit group of Vietnamese who'd served in the Provisional Recon Unit, the military arm of the infamous Phoenix project. Yes, he could put Frank in touch with a former recon man living in New Mexico. It had taken several hours to make the connection as the Viet was working and not at home. When it happened, though, all hell broke loose in Los Angeles.

Hartung's contact told the excited sergeant major he'd just been approached that morning by a recruiter from General Phong. The man, known as Phan, had asked if the former PRU commando would be interested in taking part in a job for the general that would earn him $2,500 for no more than two day's work. When the former recon specialist asked what kind of job paid such premium wages, he was told of the intended attack on a remote airstrip near the border. Hartung's new-found friend declined the offer, claiming to suffer from old wounds that made it difficult for him to walk, much less run and jump. He was thanked for his time and asked to remain silent about what he knew, as a favor to the general. Hartung had quickly thanked the former PRU, taking his address and wiring him $2,500 as a fee for the information. The payment accomplished two things. First, it ensured the veteran O&I man a link into Phong's organization, which they might have need of in the future, and second, it sealed the man's loyalty to Hartung. Should he consider double-dipping, or selling what he now knew of Frank's interest in General Phong to the drug lord, Hartung's record of payment would seal the informant's fate. It paid to be careful in the world of covert warfare, where tables as well as loyalties changed as quickly as the weather.

Utilizing maps and aerial photos of New Mexico, as well as the DEA's target folders on the area in question, the airstrip was soon located and verified. A few phone calls to Conrad Billings opened the doors and vaults of every agency Bailey needed something from, and got them the Blackhawk and its escort ship, a vision from Hell's half-acre called an "Apache." Within twelve hours SPRINGBLADE was airborne and en route, the team's intention to infiltrate the area and grab a Vietnamese drug commando for interrogation. "We'll let Phong's boys blow the shit out of the mob from Mexico, which won't break anyone's hearts on this side of the border," explained Bo during their last pre-mission briefing. "Then we'll isolate one of the Viets and grab his nasty ass. They'll be taking KIAs and WIAs anyhow, and if some poor bastard comes up MIA he'll more than likely be written off."

The all-black chopper heeled to port, lifting a huge cloud of sand from the desert's floor as it began to descend. Three feet off the deck, the team jumped from the roaring airship's skids, dropping softly into ankle-

deep sand and slogging forward until they were clear of
the rotor wash's thunder. Going to one knee and facing
outward, the team heard the Blackhawk lift off and veer
away from them, the desert suddenly silent as the ship
rapidly unassed the landing zone. They were several
klicks from the airstrip and would be in position before
dark with little effort. Thornton raised a hand and, pointing to Rowe, indicated they should get moving. Above
them the soaring heat of the day beat down at over 115
degrees Fahrenheit, reminding Bo how wise it had been
for them to double up on water before leaving the launch
site. Each man was carrying ten quarts for his personal
use, which would be only drinking. They had three LRRP
meals for the operation, plus snacks. An instructor from
the Marine Corps had been flown in to update them on
desert travel and survival, then returned to his base with
instructions to forget he'd ever left the ground. He'd
understood the drill, having spent several tours in Central
America in places where the Marines had been most
unexpected guests.

Rowe took point, setting a slow but steady pace across
the sand, which crunched and squished under his jungle
boots. Using his wrist compass, the former Beret set a
course for a distant squatting of sun-blasted rocks. On
the other side of the natural barrier lay Phong's intended
target, now guarded by a team from Canales's organization. Hartung's intelligence source had mentioned the
attack wouldn't take place until the next morning, although he wasn't sure in what form it would be. Frank
figured, given the distance and time factor, the general
would fly his troops in, probably taking the airstrip by
force and setting up an ambush for whoever was en route
from the Mexican side of the border. Rowe was to lead
the team up into the low hills, then find a RON, or

overnight spot, where they'd lay up sorry until first light.

Following his lead was Bailey, then Thornton, Silver, and finally the sergeant major. They were strung out with roughly five meters between them, tiny, almost invisible dots lost in the rough-and-tumble wilderness of the desert. Bo doubted that the airstrip's security team would have put out scouts. The walls surrounding the illicit LZ were hundreds of feet high and broken with arroyos, gullies, ravines, and plenty of fissures and cracks that could swallow a man up with the snap of an ankle or leg. Always cautious, though, he'd insisted they make the insertion at a point that was further masked from their target area by a high outcropping of broken, blasted rock from another age.

Within several hours they'd reached the base of the ridge. Thornton called a halt, the team clambering beneath an overhang that offered shade from the blistering sun. Rowe was quick to check the momentary haven for snakes and other reptiles before allowing them to take refuge from the day's heat. There were none, although there was a small pile of animal bones. Each man settled into his own space, Silver breaking out a bottle of sunscreen and passing it around after liberally dosing his face and the back of his neck with the oily liquid. Hartung tipped one of his canteens high, the act followed by each SPRINGBLADER as they quenched their thirst. Bo asked how each was feeling, concerned about sunstroke as they were moving during the worst possible part of the day for desert travel. There were no upset stomachs or headaches, both sure signs of heat exhaustion coming on in a man.

"Whaddya think, Alan? Another coupla hours of this shit, or what?" Jason pulled a small package of sweet dates from his ruck, offering them around the sweating, tired men.

"We got some humping to do yet, Jay. We're out of the sand, but what's coming is nothing but very hot rock, narrow passageways, and lots of creepy-crawly things that bite, sting, or both. I figure three more hours to the top, then maybe an hour coming down the path we spotted on the satellite photo during isolation." Rowe wiped his brow with an already damp cravat, stuffing the dark green swatch of cotton back down his shirt, where it lay coolly against his skin.

"Gonna have to put a point element out," offered Frank. "We got the possibility of running into two different sets of bad guys on this one. Phong might have come in early with his own recon team, or the Mexicans could have trail watchers out, at least up top. No sense fucking up this close to the goal line."

Thornton agreed. They were all professionals in a career field few survived unless they played hardball each and every day. They were facing a seasoned force of gunslingers who had killed before and would again. Mercy and compassion were concepts alien to the drug smuggler's character. If anything, the team would become objects of entertainment if they were captured or wounded. It had been this way since the Indian had roamed the desert, fighting the white man wherever he showed his pale face. Life and death were hard here, with only the toughest and smartest victorious.

"Let's go over the snatch one more time," said Bailey.

Bo settled himself cross-legged on the rock floor of their shelter, his CAR-15 cradled in his arms. "Once we're up top, Frank will run a visual recon with field glasses. After that, the team will work its way down the ridge and to a point roughly two hundred fifty meters away from the west side of the strip. It looks like we'll find good cover there, at least enough to set up a tight wagon-wheel perimeter.

"Figure Phong to come in as soon as there's enough light for the pilots to see the strip. We confirmed he's got at least three wartime Hueys available, all registered under a construction company the general owns. It should be a hell of a firefight, but expect the security team to get waxed. We then stand by and watch Phong's boys rip the shit outta whatever Canales sends over from Mexico. Again, it won't be much of a fight and expect a Vietnamese victory."

"That'll be a switch," Rowe said with a laugh. He was joined by the others as they exchanged observations about the overall will of the ARVN soldier to take it belly-to-belly with his counterpart, the VC or NVA. There'd been exceptions, of course, but not enough to wipe out the stigma attached to the South Vietnamese Army as a whole.

After they'd quieted, Bo continued. "We'll take our man based on how fate treats us. Alan and Jay are the snatch team, the rest of us security. Once they locate a likely target, we'll let 'em move, providing cover as best we can. The target secured, we move him to a safe place and pop several cc's of walkie-talkie juice into him. Frank handles the interrogation, then terminates the source. Any questions?" Alan raised a bent index finger. "Yeah, Al, what ya got?"

"Bo, is it absolutely necessary to kill the man? Can't we just leave him, or let him go after he's come to? That's murder we're talking about if I remember my law."

"We're a sanctioned project under presidential order. We need information and we need it fast. If we're fortunate enough to snatch someone who knows something we can use, he's got to be removed. Let him loose out here and he'll probably die anyway. Leave him and there's no guarantee some animal won't come along and do our job for us. We could take him back, but . . ."

"We could do that, Bo." It was Hartung. "Shit, we'll have room in the chopper, and Calvin here can put the slug on ice until we've finished the job. I'll do the final number if it's necessary, but . . ."

"But if there's a way to get around it, we should use it, right?" The team stared at each other for a moment, then nodded as one at their One-Zero. If Bo wanted the man terminated, they'd do it, no questions asked. It was his decision to make, his job as a team leader to watch out for their overall security and safety. Thornton weighed the odds, the benefits, and made up his mind in an instant. "Okay. We pull everything we can outta the asshole then tote his funky ass to the PZ. He'll be Al's and Jay's responsibility after Frank finishes with him. I'll notify the chopper we'll be one extra as it's inbound. I'm not into killing for killing's sake, so we'll take a chance to make our mamas proud."

Heads nodded as smiles broke across the men's faces. They were walking a fine line regardless of sanctions or contracts coming from the Oval Office, and they knew it. The important thing was to take only those missions that they could justify to a man, and to carry them out as cleanly and professionally as possible. After all, they would have to live with the results of their actions long after SPRINGBLADE was disbanded, if they themselves lived to see that day. Each of them had been around the world enough times to know there was only one accountability worth worrying about, and that was to the Man Upstairs. Although they'd racked up an impressive

head-count over the span of their collective career, it
wouldn't do to start chalking up black marks just for the
perverted hell of it.

"Okay, I've done my liberal bullshit for the day. Let's
get it on!" Thornton peered out from under the massive
shale overhang, checking the area around them before
scrambling back into the sunlight. His rifle at the ready,
Bo stood watch as the rest of the team took their positions. Rowe stayed on point, a light pair of canvas gloves
protecting his hands as he began working his way into
the jagged confusion of broken rock that faced them.
Alan would work well ahead of the main body from here
on out, marking his progress as he went, as much a piece
of bait as anything else. It would be up to him to find
"them" first, then to either pull back or engage. They
would have the sun at their backs, which meant anyone
up top would have it in their eyes. It was an important
advantage.

The climb was un-fucking-real. Rowe watched his
gloves literally fall apart before his eyes as he hauled
himself up the steep rock, grabbing for handholds and
scrambling for footholds where there appeared to be
none. Several times he nearly grabbed ahold of a long,
angry rattler whose beaded tail was stiff with the excitement of ramming its venom-filled fangs into soft, yield-
ing flesh. Alan hated snakes, although he was not afraid
of them. Behind him the team struggled to keep up,
Hartung often working out on the sides so he could maintain an eagle's eye on the lone point man's progress.
Rowe was completely exposed in the position he was in.
Frank would have to pull double duty to make sure the
man didn't get whacked by default.

Thornton was sweating like a hog. The uniform that
had been so comfortable in the chopper was now soaked,

huge damp patches forming under his arms and between his legs. His fingers and forearms were stiff with the exertion of his climb, and Bo wished he'd brought the same kind of gloves he'd seen Alan slip on after their rest break; his fingertips were raw and bleeding. How the hell do I get myself into these things, wondered Thornton as he watched a huge silver-gray lizard streak across a portion of almost verticle rock. I ought to be with Linda in Paris, screwing her silly and enjoying my retirement. Hell, we've made enough off the first four missions to sit back and slowly go senile in comfort. What the fuck am I doing three hundred feet off the deck with one more go-to-hell firefight ahead of me? Bo struggled over a small outcropping, turning to wave at Hartung, who was just beginning the pitch Thornton had finished. Fucking Frank! He'd earned his down time more than any three of them put together. Heavy Hook was the love of his life, a business that the sergeant major had built from the ground up as Thornton wandered around Oregon looking for a spot of land to build a house on. It hadn't started out that way; both men had been committed to opening a dive shop in San Diego that would take advantage of their backgrounds and connections. Thornton just couldn't stay still, and then along came that shit-for-brains squid with his offer of a little action, a little cash, and some fine feelings. Hartung didn't need to be here. Hell, none of them needed this shit!

"He's nearly on top. I can see him waving just past that big mutherfucking boulder off to your left." Calvin clambered up past Bo, finding a shallow lip on which to perch while he caught his breath.

Thornton looked up and waved, Rowe's face barely visible to him. "I may hang this shit up after we shut

Phong down, Cal.'' The warrior king unsnapped his canteen flap, dragging the jet-black container free and offering his friend the first warm pull of sweet water it held.

Bailey gratefully accepted, pouring a thoughtful measure of the life-giving liquid down his throat after washing it around in his mouth first. Handing the canteen back, he spoke. ''Figured sooner or later I'd hear you say that. This is as good a place as any, I suppose.'' Glancing around, Calvin took in the desert's splendor, its rich colors as the sun began drifting downward, painting the landscape in deep tones of pink, red, orange, and yellow. ''Damn pretty up here. Hard to believe we can't be enjoying it under other circumstances.''

Thornton nodded. ''Exactly my thoughts, Cal. How many dragons more will we be expected to slay? Frank— bless his leather-bound soul—should be in San Diego ringing up the till on his retirement and humping some eager middle-class hogette instead of that ruck down there. Jason's got a good deal brewing with his art gallery, and Linda's overseas shopping for our house while I'm . . .''

''While you're sweating your ass off playing soldier, is that it?''

''Fucking-A that's it! We're not doing anything more than cleaning up what never should have been spilled to begin with. Somebody upstairs says, 'Well, this is pretty fucked, so let's dispense with the law and just kill the sons of bitches,' and off we go. I dunno, Cal. Back there I was all geared up to just whack our POW and be done with it. You guys squared me away, started me thinking, that's all.''

Bailey popped a cigarette out of its pack, looking to Thornton, who nodded an okay. If they hadn't been spotted yet by all the racket their climbing was making, a smoke wouldn't do any more harm. Lighting the cigarette with a silver Zippo, a gift from his last SEAL team, Bailey blew a long rush of smoke from his lungs and sighed. "I hate these things, you know, just can't seem to get away from them. Anyhow, I hear what you're saying and I can't help but agree."

Thornton looked at the sweaty agent with surprise. "Hey, you're supposed to be restoring my waning confidence, pal. Don't fuck up and start telling me I'm thinking straight. Billings'll have your young ass if you lose this team to stuff like 'humanity' and 'human dignity.'"

Bailey laughed lightly, a sudden breeze pulling the sound from his lips. "Shit, fuck Billings and the horse he rode in on. You guys want to pull the plug after this gig, that's cool with me. SPRINGBLADE was meant to be a stopgap measure anyhow. But your boys are so damn good at what they do, it's easier to sanction a mission than to look for deeper answers. If you shut it down—and you have that option—they'll just build another team or plug in a SLAM platoon, period."

"Real fucking imaginative aren't they?" commented Bo.

"Not really," answered Bailey, his cigarette burned down to its filter. "Remember, they're politicians." Both men laughed silently, then began to ready themselves for the final ascent, to where Rowe and Silver were already waiting for them.

"Let's get it on, squid. We've wasted enough time jacking our jaws, and besides, there's a bunch of folks on the other side of this rockpile that are just *dying* to meet us!"

"Airborne and Amen," offered Frank Hartung, whose exertions had brought him up even with his two friends.

"Now shut the fuck up and get your asses in gear!"

"Roger that, Sergeant Major!" said both men, the bottoms of their boots all Frank could see as they scampered up the remaining incline like two kids on a rope.

# CHAPTER

# 9

Long trails of sunlight were carefully exploring their way across the darkness of the morning, their fingers like veins of pure gold against the chilly morning's blackness. The lone Mexican on watch was shivering despite his thick coat and heavy wool blanket, envying his friends who were rolled up tight in their lightweight down bags. He longed to start a fire, its flames both a companion and a source of heat to ward off the desert's cold. It wouldn't have to be a large fire, perhaps one the size of a coffee can's lid, placed in a pit hand-dug into the loose sand so the embers wouldn't give their position away. The Mexican dismissed the thought with a wave of his hand. They were under strict instructions from Canales: no fires during the night and stay out of sight during the day. The boss wants this *cabron* pretty badly, he mused to himself as the sun began arching into the sky. Soon one of their old C-47 cargo planes would be landing, its

guts filled with some hard boys who would be moving
northward towards Taos when two chartered helicopters
arrived later that afternoon. Canales was one pissed off
*jefe* to send this large a hit team after one Chinaman, or
whatever the hell he was.

Pulling himself off the warmth of the huge, flat rock
he'd been sitting on, the guard walked quietly to where
the others slept. One by one he roused them, shaking
them and talking in his native tongue. Only the Mexicans
had been sent out to secure the plane's landing strip, the
few gringos and Europeans Canales kept on the payroll
refusing to spend even one day frying their brains out in
the middle of a New Mexican desert. At first this had
bothered the guard, whose name was Francisco although
he was known as Paco. Later, though, after they'd been
dropped off by the same plane coming in with the main
body in a very few hours, he'd been pleased the others
had stayed back. At least Paco and his Mexican brothers
wouldn't have to put up with the endless stupid jokes
the mercenaries made them the butt of, and they could
converse in Spanish, a skill only a few of the foreigners
possessed with any degree of understanding. Fuck 'em!
Paco understood the desert and loved its isolation and
simplicity. It took hardy men—*hombres con cojones*—
to live in the desert. Screw the others; they would make
do and greet their dainty asses when the plane arrived.

By the time they'd dragged themselves out from the
accumulated warmth of their down-filled cocoons, Paco
had a brisk fire going beneath the protection of several
large pieces of shale he'd stacked so they formed a crude
shelter to cook under. A well-used coffee pot was beginning to bubble, the Mexican slowly sifting a handful
of rich coffee into the boiling water. When the brew was
finished, he would remove the can from the fire, then

pour just a bit of cold water into it to settle the grounds. It was an old trick used by the *vaqueros* in years past, taught to Paco by his father's father.

When the coffee was ready, they gathered around the tiny fire, holding their tin or plastic cups in hand. There were but ten of them, heavily armed and with supplies for only three days. They were smugglers, murderers, robbers, and thieves. There were at least three rapists in the band, and one homosexual. All in all they were a dangerous, albeit motley, lot of very bad men. A thick joint was fired up by one huge bandit, its heady vapor mixing with the coffee's. After taking two huge hits, the Mexican passed the finger-thick cigarette on to one of his companions, who sucked greedily at the hand-rolled tube. None of them were worried about perhaps having to fight stoned; in fact many of them had fought their best battles that way. Dope was often used to strip away the fear of death or mutilation during combat. There were limits, of course, but these men had yet to find out what those were. Soon the smell of eggs and bacon frying rose up with the sizzling of a wad of cooking grease in a huge frying pan. The band's laughter mixed easily with the cooking fire's smoke, giving the scene an appearance of being nothing more than a overnight camping trip made up of good old boys out for a good old time.

The sun was cresting the tops of the ridges when they heard the sound of engines in the distance. As one, they checked their watches, commenting among themselves that Canales must have sent either the plane or the choppers early. With no radio to communicate with the aircraft or Canales himself, they were at the mercy of any changes the *jefe* might wish to impose on the original plan. Not a one of them was worried, although there was the slight possibility the planes were from the DEA's growing air force.

Slowly taking up their positions, rifles and submachine guns in hand, they turned their eyes southward. The burned-out steel drums had been rolled out of the way upon their arrival, now serving as makeshift tables for the endless card games that had taken place after the plane had dropped them off. A few of the gunmen had strung shelter-halves between the rocks as protection from the sun, storing their rucksacks as well as themselves beneath them. These would come down once the main party was safely on the ground. The throbbing of turbines grew louder as ten pair of eyes strained to catch sight of the iron birds. Paco recognized the engines as belonging to helicopters, a thought that bothered him because Canales possessed no such aircraft on his side of the border. Perhaps the choppers for them had gotten their information wrong, he thought. If it were the helos, they could all position themselves early on for the best seats going in to Taos. That simple pleasure would be reward in itself for the time spent idle in the wilderness.

From the end of the rough dirt strip came a shout. Indeed they were helicopters, the buglike hulls clearly visible as they dropped down the side of the farthest ridge and began their approach at well over sixty knots per hour. Excited voices began calling to each other as the three slicks hammered their way across the desert's floor, their frames less than fifty feet above the broken rock and endless sand that made up the blasted, scorched surface. Paco searched his drug-muddled mind. Hadn't they been told there would be only *two* choppers?

The Mexican watched as the first airship suddenly began to outdistance its comrades, flying fast and low until it roared down the length of the strip just above their heads. Paco could see that its interior was full of men, the bottoms of their boots clearly visible from where they were hanging out the doorless sides of the chopper. Everyone else was waving and yelling, raising their weapons high in the air in a hearty welcome to the new-comers. Some had even run out onto the strip itself, turning to watch the remaining two ships as they began their approach.

It was then that Paco's mind registered what was wrong. Boots! There was supposed to be only *pilots* on the choppers, not men! Canales had no helicopters in his fleet, only light aircraft and transports. It was a transport that would be bringing in *men*, the choppers ferrying them out again! This was a trap! Throwing his well-worn AR-15 to his shoulder the Mexican began to fire wildly at the nose of the second chopper, the sharp *craaack* of the lightweight assault rifle silencing his friends, who turned to see what fool was shooting. "It's a trick, you idiots!" the rifleman yelled as he vainly tried to keep the enlarging bulb of the Huey's nose atop his front sight post. "Shoot them down! It's a fucking gringo trick!"

From behind him the Mexican heard a barrage of rifle fire erupt, realizing as the first rounds hit him below the knees that they were coming from the deck of the first chopper, now behind them. Falling to one knee and roll-ing, Paco ended up on his back, where he placed the AR between his knees and emptied its magazine at the hov-ering black bug. He was startled to see one of the chop-per's occupants fly forward and out of the airship, landing heavily on the rocks twenty feet below. An angry stream of high velocity hornets swarmed out from the Huey's interior, impacting all around the wounded Mexican but failing to find his once-again moving body.

The second ship was over the strip, both sides alive

with outgoing automatic weapons fire as the Vietnamese inside unloaded everything they had on the hapless security team below. One man was caught in a hail of rifle fire, his body jerking and leaping as several magazines' worth of 5.56 firepower tore into his lean frame, shredding muscle and tissue into bloody confetti. In a flash of steel and lead the Huey was gone, the pilot looking for altitude in order to avoid the cliffs Thornton's team had climbed the day before. Already, the third gunship had taken its place, and three more Mexicans were slaughtered as the Viets opened up from less than ten feet off the sand.

Paco was into his third magazine. The first chopper was now on the opposite side of the strip, flying slowly while its gunners fired away at the now prone figures of the security team. The second Huey assumed a similar flight pattern where the first had been when it nailed the wounded Mexican, both choppers flying a lazy 360-degree orbit as the third rocketed out and over the northern cliff face. Drawing a steady bead on the second bird's open doorway, Paco squeezed off five rounds. He pounded his fist against the sand in triumph as another intruder grabbed at his face, dropping his rifle, which slid out of the aircraft despite someone trying to grab it. The Mexican dragged himself over to the body of a man he recognized as Emilio. He'd been caught full in the face with a burst of gunfire that had reduced his already ugly features to a nightmare of bone and shredded beef. Saving what little ammunition he had left, the Mexican tugged two full magazines of .223 hollow points from Emilio's canvas pouches, jamming one of them into the AR and the other into his breast pocket.

Peering over the corpse, he watched in anger as two of his companions leaped to their feet and ran for the distant safety of the cliff's rocky base. The slicks had completed a full orbit, and as soon as the two appeared, the second gun platform broke out of its pattern and zoomed down on top of the sprinters, leveling out beside them so the gunners inside could take careful aim. Paco watched his amigos disintegrate as eight magazines of various calibers tore into their bodies. Chancing being discovered, the Mexican whipped his rifle over the body of Emilio and ripped off half a magazine at the slow-flying Huey. This time he watched two of the invaders collapse, one falling free and bouncing several feet in the air as the aircraft reacted to the unseen sniper's accuracy.

Suddenly the ground around Paco disappeared as huge clouds of sand and stone were whipped into a frenzy around the prostrate man. Rolling onto his back, the Mexican found himself staring at the soft underbelly of the third chopper, which had joined its two sister ships. Before he could bring his rifle to bear, the hard-flying pilot slipped the airframe to the right, exposing a firing squad's worth of gun barrels. Paco began screaming as he lifted the AR with one hand, aiming his own barrel at the wall of oriental faces glaring angrily down at him from their aluminum haven. He was successful in getting two rounds off before being spattered like a bloated insect against the sand. Hundreds of flashing lights went off before his eyes as the Viets power-sawed their way through his body using 5.56 teeth. The roar of the guns overpowered even the helo's turbine engine, drowning Paco in an ocean of cordite and flame. He hadn't seen yet another of Phong's soldiers bite into one of his bullets, the other punching through the chopper's thin roof and exiting without any further damage.

The first Huey set down, its cargo erupting from the

doorways and running pell-mell across the strip to take up positions on the opposite side. The second ship in trail took the northern end of the field, dropping its load and quickly regaining the air to search for any survivors. After erasing Paco from the high desert chalkboard, the third and final Huey shifted its weight across and to the center of the LZ, setting down and cutting its engine while a squad's worth of Vietnamese began systematically searching the bodies of the Mexicans scattered about the flat expanse.

The remainder of the operation was pretty cut and dried. Squad leaders took count of their men and equipment, ensuring that the dead were policed up and covered off to one side of the strip. The Vietnamese assault leader was highly pissed off at his initial losses, all which had been inflicted by Paco's skill and luck. They'd taken only one wounded, his injuries so severe the man's squad leader hastily dispatched him with a single bullet to the brain. The pilots were responsible for checking their aircraft for damage, each walking around his bird inspecting its thin skin for holes or tears. The Huey was a strange aircraft, capable of soaking up tremendous combat damage or being shot out of the sky with a single well-placed round. They needed all three birds to get the attacking force back to civilization after the hit on Canales went down. Upon completing their inspection, the crews would shuttle the choppers several klicks out, putting them down in a hidden valley they'd spotted from the air on their way in. Once the Viet ground commander informed them of the successful second part of Phong's plan, they'd fly in to scoop up the surviving Viets and head for home.

Within twenty minutes the strip had been cleared of its human debris, ten of the Viets putting up a makeshift encampment and posing as the Mexican security team. It was assumed that the expected aircraft would simply make its approach and land, given there was no radio found among the Mexicans' gear, or any kind of visual signal prepared. The Viet in charge positioned two LAW rocket teams at each end of the LZ, with a supporting M60 light machine gun assigned to each group. That ate up what manpower he had available, the deaths during the early morning assault having depleted his reserves. As per Phong's instructions, they would wait until the plane taxied to the end of the runway and began its slow turn before hitting it with the LAWs. Whichever rocket team was still armed would immediately reposition itself to engage the plane's fuselage, the LMGs instructed to expend everything they'd brought into the wreckage until ordered to cease firing.

Answering a shout from behind him, the Viet was pleased to see six Mexican heads, including Paco's, plunged one by one down upon a presharpened wooden spike. The other four skulls had been too badly damaged to do anything with, due to the battering they'd taken from the airborne marksmen. Six would send the appropriate message, thought the ground commander to himself. He doubted there would be anything left after they engaged the plane with rockets and tracer fire. It would burn until nothing was left but bits of twisted steel and aluminum, a fitting memorial to the general's brilliance.

Instructing his squad leaders with curt orders, he released them to carry out their duties. He wanted at least one team of two men moving beyond their perimeter, just in case one of the Mexicans had escaped. To accomplish this, he cut loose his RTO and one other, feeling that radio communications wouldn't be a problem for him to handle as long as the set was with him at the makeshift CP. Glancing at his watch, he noted that they were right on schedule, the plane from Mexico due in anytime now. He was not impressed with the shoddy efforts made by the Mexican security team to prepare and defend the landing strip; obviously they were amateurs at their jobs, mere bumpkins at the art of land warfare.

They'd deserved to die. Idiots! Fools! Scum!

Settling himself in the sand, the Viet lifted a cup of still-hot coffee to his lips. He'd found the pot atop one of the gasoline drums that had been left standing when the gunfire ended. Sipping at the strong brew, he smacked his lips in appreciation. At least one of the dead men had possessed a commendable skill, even if it was only being able to make a good cup of coffee!

# CHAPTER

# 10

"Holy shit!" exclaimed Silver as he watched the final moments of Paco's low-life existence ticking off. "Who went and taught the ARVN to fight like that! They coulda kicked ass back in the war if they'd fired and maneuvered like these guys are doing."

The team was hunkered down in a narrow, winding arroyo that cut its way from the cliffs climbed the day before down to within two hundred fifty meters of the dirt landing strip formerly occupied by Canales's ten-man force. Each SPRINGBLADER was well camouflaged, their uniforms now dry and speckled with bits of desert vegetation carefully added to further break up their distinctive outlines. Thornton's order to put out claymores resulted in a tight circle of steel protecting their position, each mine linked to the next with a stretch of det-cord. If discovered, they would simply blow the mines and start running, calling for the evac ship to meet them at a predesignated spot half a klick away. Bo felt confident that they wouldn't need to E&E, as long as the snatch went down quickly and with little fanfare.

"They got something worth fighting for this time around." The speaker was Hartung, an unlit cigar clamped between his teeth in the side of his mouth. "Back in the war the everyday Vietnamese soldier knew he was pretty much nothing in the eyes of his commanders. They got ripped off, underpaid, and sent out to die on operations which were poorly planned and often badly executed. What the hell did they have to look forward to?

"Now they're in America, working for a local legend who was one of the few to care about his men. He pays them good money, takes care of their families, and gives them the respect they never had. Sure they fight good; look at the bums kicking the shit outta those dope-smokin' fools! The trouble is the war is over, and they fucking lost it. It wasn't American mistakes, or lack of American support. It was a lack of feeling their country was worth fighting for at the grass roots level, plain and simple."

"So now they're getting their own by running dope into the country that took them in? Fuck that bullshit! I know too many honest, hardworking Vietnamese, as well as half a hundred other minorities who are busting their asses to make the American Dream come true. These dudes are the exception, man. Not the fucking rule." Silver cast a look of pure hatred at the busy raiders, who were now dragging the dead from both sides off the LZ.

"You and Rowe get your shit together, we gotta be ready to move in on one of these rock apes as soon as one makes himself available.'' Thornton lowered the field glasses, wiping a heavy beading of sweat from his brow. ''What's next, Frank?''

The veteran looked over at where Bo lay, a gleam in his eye as he spoke. Hartung was a top field tactician, with more time behind a rifle's butt stock than any three decent officers Thornton could remember. Frank's mind was a computer when it came to working through probable scenarios, and Bo counted on Hartung's accuracy to make his own decisions as a One-Zero for this particular team. ''Gotta get the choppers airborne and outta here before the plane comes in, that's first on the agenda. They'll move 'em off a coupla klicks or so, set 'em down and wait until they get the word to extract. We gotta think about being forced to E&E; no way we can hope to evade an airborne platform in this terrain.''

''Good point,'' said Thornton. Looking at the team, he changed part of their planning, taking the choppers into account as suggested by the sergeant major. ''We get blown, take the arroyo back up into the cliffs. We'll link up there and call in our own air assets to push these boys off us. With an AH-64 in the air, those slick jockeys will turn tail and boogie most ric-tic.''

After the team acknowledged Thornton's announcement, Frank continued. ''I saw LAWs being extended a moment ago, and they gotta a few LMGs, too. If it were me, I'd just rocket the bird when it reached the apex of its taxi pattern, then gun every swinging Richard who might still be alive inside. No fuss, no muss. A clean hit and a clean getaway. End of story.''

''Does it have to be a clean getaway?'' asked Rowe.

''Whatta ya mean, Al? We sure as shit can't take Phong's toads on with these popguns of ours.''

"I don't think we have to consider that option, Frank,"
responded the suddenly enthusiastic commando. "We're
to let Phong take out the Canales mob, no?" They all
agreed; that fact was made clear before they launched.
"So, they get their rocks off and the choppers over there
make the extraction window, no problem. From what I
remember from our briefings from Cal here, the DEA
and National Guard run overflights through this area
pretty frequently. True?" Bailey nodded, a glimmer of
what Alan was getting at starting to burst into flames
inside his head. "So why not let Phong's people get
airborne, then put the Apache on their asses? That bad
boy will have been sitting out in the hot desert long
enough to want to do some serious flying, and the slicks
will be no match for what's on board the '64. Phong
blows Canales away, we snatch a POW, the Apache
whips a little ass on the general's home team, and no
one's the wiser."

"Just bad luck on the Viets' part, eh? Wrong time,
wrong place kinda thing," murmured Silver. "I like it,
I fucking-A like it a lot! Whatta ya say, Bo?"

Thornton cracked a smile, caked dirt from around his
mouth breaking free and dropping onto his fatigue shirt
as the taut skin crinkled and twisted into a grin at
Alan's suggestion. "I'm for it," he said. "How about
it, Cal?"

Bailey nodded in agreement. "Let me touch base with
our air assets before this POW play kicks off. We gotta
justify to the Congress all the big bucks an Apache costs
anyhow. Besides, everything's been going the general's
way lately. Maybe it's time to dust his nuts a bit."

Five minutes later the deal was done. Ten klicks away,
the Apache's two-man crew was hurriedly conducting
their preflight checks, arming the multiple-option arsenal

possessed by the AH-64 and jabbering crazily between each other about how best to blow three low-flying Hueys out of the air in a single pass.

It was a great day to be flying.

# CHAPTER

## 11

The C-47 made one pass over the strip, the pilot encouraged by the wildly waving men below. Inside the cramped aircraft were thirty-five of Canales's best gunners, all hard men with equally hard won reputations. Scattered among the Latins on board were eleven foreigners, seven Americans and five Europeans. Out of this team came the element meant to hunt Phong down once the massive show of force infiltrated Taos. There was one sniper team made up of Americans, and a three-man bomb team consisting of one Irishman and two Brits. The rest of the mob were charged with disrupting Phong's organization on its home turf. Canales had had enough of the Viet's arrogant behavior.

Landing gear down, the plane drifted into its perfect lineup with the strip's center. The crew, both Frenchmen, had put their craft down on this and a dozen other dirt runways over the border so many times they'd lost count.

They were professional smugglers, pilots whose skill was in high demand by the international dope trade. Loads couldn't be sold if they couldn't be brought to market, and good flyers were worth their weight in gold. Adjusting their drift, the copilot joined hands with his senior as together they grasped the huge levers controlling the twin engines powering their flight. Landings were the toughest part of flying, requiring exact coordination on the controls by both men to be successful. As they leveled out, the desert flying by at over one hundred twenty knots per hour, both lost sight of the welcoming party that had been out in force just minutes before.

The first rocket team hastily abandoned their position, urging the machine gunner to follow them as they ran pell-mell toward the north end of the strip. Their secondary position was already prepared, dug in and fortified with large hunks of rock by order of their commander. It would be their job to complete the destruction of the aircraft once the team at the other end crippled it with their two LAWs. Accuracy would play an important part in the success of their ambush, the LAW being somewhat difficult to guide on target unless one was totally at ease with it. Panting and running at full tilt along the edge of the LZ, the Vietnamese reached their open pit seconds before the big plane started its turn at the end of the field. The machine gunner popped his bipod open, slamming the twenty-six–pound weapon onto the ground and charging the bolt in two well-rehearsed motions. He had over three hundred rounds available, with the rocket team carrying two hundred more in their rucks. Jamming the hard black butt into the pocket of his shoulder, the gunner laid the heavy front blade sight directly on the cockpit's centerline.

The pilot had nearly completed his slow turn when the first rocket blew his tail rudder off. Thinking they'd hit an unseen boulder, the pilot immediately feathered his engines, slowing them even more. The second LAW whipped out of a camouflaged crevice, punching its way into the crowded cabin just above the plane's right wing joint. The ensuing explosion killed half the men from the center beam forward, secondary blasts from grenades and light-weapons ammunition adding to the fury of the assault.

Both crew members had time only to point at the blinking muzzle flash of the M60 before the cockpit's window shattered into a thousand screaming slivers of thick glass. Round after 7.62 round crashed into the pilot's and copilot's bodies, carving out huge hunks of still-living flesh as quarts of hot, steamy blood sprayed about the interior of the cramped compartment. The plane began to yaw to the right when the first LAW from the backup team roared downrange. It impacted against the cowling of the starboard engine, blowing the wing clear away in a thunderous blast of fire and fragments. The remaining rocketman held his fire, watching as the crippled relic slued to a stop, the front nose wheel collapsing under the violent shuddering of the airframe as it thudded to a halt.

Taking careful aim, the Viet plunged the rubber-encased trigger downward, closing his eyes as the massive roar of the rocket ripped its way past his head. A shout of congratulations erupted from his teammates as the warhead slapped wickedly into the plane's rear, tearing it completely free and spilling a massed ball of living and half-living bodies onto the dirt below. Suddenly it was a contest between the two light machine guns as to who would reap the greater harvest. Each gunner sent

long streams of red tracer into the struggling mass of
flesh and bone, their aim assisted by their now rocketless
comrades, who shouted adjustments at the gunners,
whose eyes were blinded by the clouds of gun smoke
their weapons were emitting. From the flanks came the
high-pitched popping of half a dozen M16s, the Viet
ground commander and his support team getting their
licks in. Three minutes later it was all over, the infantry
on line and advancing toward the wildly burning plane
and its stinking innards.

Thornton nodded, sending both Silver and Rowe over
the lip of their stony sanctuary in a half-crouch. Both
road runners raced toward an outcropping of rock ten
meters to their front, sliding down behind it as Hartung
covered their progress with his CAR-15. Bailey and Bo
were moving rapidly down the arroyo, anxious to provide
a flanking element should things go to shit. Reaching a
sharp bend in the ragged cut, they propped themselves
over the crumbling trench's lip and watched the final
agonizing moments of the gallant old aircraft's life.

"What a waste of a perfectly good airplane," said
Calvin. "Those old 47s can go anywhere and do anything. Pity this one ended up in the hands of a dope
merchant."

"Watch the front, squid!" reminded Bo. "Those two
yahoos we spotted nosing around the back forty have
dropped outta sight. Rowe's getting ready to move again,
so lock and load!"

Bailey squinted through the round opening of his rear
sight as Alan low-crawled forward, his head bobbing and
weaving as he searched for their target. A minute later
Jason followed, his progress covered by Rowe's carbine.
"Where the hell did those two go?" worried the narc.

"They were sitting there all nice and pretty, popping magazines by the shitload at those poor assholes in the plane. Where are they now?"

Alan pulled Silver up next to him, the slight shale wall they were behind barely hiding the two men from sight. "Damn! This is where we last spotted those jerks, where the hell they go?"

Panting with the heat and blast-furnace jolts of adrenaline, Jason pointed to a shallow trench much like the one they'd been standing in earlier. "There . . . the pukes slipped into that trench and are probably hanging out somewhere in it taking a smoke break."

Giving each other an encouraging eye, both commandos raced across the small expanse of open ground separating them from the trench, jumping feet first into the shoulder-deep ditch. Ten feet away the two Vietnamese leaped up, cigarettes falling from their mouths as they gaped in surprise at two desert-clad invaders. Silver watched as one man dropped his rifle and fled down the earthen corridor, sprinting after him as the second Viet tried to crawl out of the trench. "Take this one!" he yelled over his shoulder, dropping his own carbine as its barrel and stock banged off the sides of the long grave. Unsheathing the Hartsfield *khukuri*, Jason bounded after his prey, a macabre interest in seeing how well the blade performed urging him after the fleeing soldier.

Rowe leaped at the remaining soldier's lower legs, catching him in a lineman's grip just as he was about to escape. With a sharp twist, Alan turned the man onto his back, dragging him into the sand-filled moat, where they both collapsed in a heap of kicking and scratching. Rowe saw the Viet yank a short-bladed hunting knife from its sheath on his pistol belt, the darkened blade glinting evilly in the glare of the searing sun above them. Long furrows of light skin appeared on Alan's face as rivers of sweat washed away the layer of powdered dirt that had built up over the last several hours of waiting. Whipping a handful of gritty sand into his enemy's eyes, Rowe aimed a snap kick at the man's groin, missing as the Viet turned and caught the powerful blow with his hip. Alan followed the man as he fell from the kick's impact, resisting the urge to whip the big Applegate smatchet out and behead the filthy shitbird where he lay.

The fallen man shook his head just as Rowe's hands latched onto the front of his uniform shirt. Grabbing the SPRINGBLADER by the wrists, the Viet squeezed and twisted them together so that Alan was forced to release him or face having the fragile bones broken. "You son of a bitch!" whispered Alan as he fast-stepped back away from the Viet.

"Fuck you, too, you son of a Japanese whore!" retorted the man.

"Chinese, you rat-sucking spawn of a slut's womb! I'm motherfucking Chinese and don't you forget it!" With that, Rowe, who'd hated being called a Japanese ever since he'd learned the difference between the two races from his father, leaped forward. He threw chops and kicks that dazzled the Viet, forcing the man backward until he fell in a heap at Alan's feet. This time the veteran huntsman waited until the downed soldier tried to sit up, dropping suddenly to one knee and snapping a withering forward palm strike against the Viet's forehead as his eyes were beginning to focus. The blow snapped the dazed trooper's head back, dropping him for the count. Rowe had already jerked the smatchet from its Cordura sheath, intending to land a blow against the man's temple

with its blunted butt had the palm strike failed to blow
his circuits out.

Sheathing the massive blade, Alan quickly checked
around him to be sure he hadn't been joined by nonfriend-
lies. Secure, he removed a pair of black polymer hand-
cuffs from his right cargo pocket and snapped them
around the prisoner's wrists. He removed his cravat from
around his neck and tied the man's ankles together. Finished, Rowe squatted to await Silver's return.

Jason plowed after the Viet, slipping twice and slamming
his knees into the rocky earth so hard it brought grunts
of pain to his lips both times. He could hear the sound
of rapid footsteps just ahead of him, aware also that the
arroyo was growing deeper and wider as they ran along
it. Wary of running headlong into a one-man ambush,
the former recon ranger forced himself to slow down,
keeping a steady pace with his quarry as the man searched
for a way out of the ever-lengthening channel. Without
warning they were face-to-face, a slim-bladed Glock bay-
onet held low in front of the Viet as he determined to
take his pursuer belly-to-belly.

"Well, well, well," exclaimed Jason as he eyed the
tiny knife in mild amusement. "Looks like Mr. 'I Fling
Poo' has a toy he wants to try out. Is that how it is, you
skinny little weasel?"

The Viet didn't take the bait. Instead he shuffled forward, his eyes bouncing off Silver's *khukuri* as he registered the size and power of the much larger knife. With
a snarl he leaped forward, the knife whipping tight figure-
eights that could go either into a man's face, throat, belly,
or groin. Silver moved forward, sidestepping the sizzling
blade and twisting so he could bring the *khukuri* down
hard across the man's upper forearm. The blade sliced

through the whipcordlike flesh and bone as if it didn't exist. As the Viet began to understand his loss, Jason continued moving as a long stream of crimson liquid burst from the severed arteries and veins now protruding from the open amputation. Stepping behind the man, Silver brought the ancient knife from Nepal rearward, raising it high over his head and slamming it down so that the razor-keen edge bit deeply into the stunned soldier's neck. The *khukuri* never stopped moving, severing tissue, gristle, tendons, blood pipelines, and finally the upper portion of the spinal column as if they were made from rice paper. The Viet's head rolled sideways, releasing a gout of rich arterial blood high into the air as the man's heart beat at a furious pace, pumping itself empty within seconds. As the mutilated body slumped onto the now-sodden desert soil, Silver glared at the dead man's decapitated features. Without a word he sheathed the *khukuri*, unholstering the Glock at his side and loping back up the ravine to where he hoped Alan Rowe would be waiting with a live POW.

Frank Hartung checked the prisoner out, wafting a broken vial of ammonia under the man's nose, which brought him to in a fit of snorts and coughs. Satisfied, the sergeant major once again checked the Viet's bonds, then asked him a few basic questions in his native language. There was no response. Hartung shrugged at Bo, who gave a rigid thumbs-up, then turned to rejoin the rest of the team on watch.

Frank extracted a fully loaded hypodermic needle from its place in his first aid kit. Holding the needle aloft, he pushed a few drops of amber-colored liquid out through the narrow needle's nose, then suddenly whipped the hypo deep into the now wide-awake POW's upper arm.

The Viet struggled for a few moments, his movements slowing as the double dose of truth serum reached his brain's cortex. After that, all went well, with lazy, slurred answers bubbling up from the soldier, who turned out to be the ground forces commander's RTO. After ten minutes of rapid questioning, Frank wrapped up his field interrogation by scribbling some quick notes into his pocket-size squad leader's notebook.

"You finished?" It was Bo, anxious to get the next phase of the operation going, as the Vietnamese ground force was obviously preparing to leave the AO.

"Roger that. It was Phong who hit the Colombian, three-man team that's en route back from Florida. Canales is the front man for the rest of the Latin connection, so he's trying to look tough. After today he's going to look like shit on a stick. The general is moving quickly, planning to take out three major caravans within the next seventy-two hours. We'll learn more from Sleeping Ugly here, once we get him back to the DEA launch site."

Bo grunted. "Nice work, Frank. Bailey's calling in our transportation; we'll lift after the NVA pull out. The Apache is standing by on station. He'll interdict once the bad guys are clear of us. Should be quite a show; I've heard the '64 is one mean mother in the air."

Hartung smiled at Thornton's unconscious reference to Phong's force as being NVA. Shit, they might as well be, he thought as together they gagged and dragged the still-babbling prisoner deeper into their protective gutter. Fucking NVA woulda done that plane just the way these boys did. Boom, boom, boom. Gun the survivors, leave the bodies as proof of purchase, and head for the rear area with one helluva hard-on for the little woman back home.

Bailey broke the sergeant major's train of thought with

his announcement that the Apache's TADS system had just picked up three aircraft inbound for their location. TADS allowed the gunship to search out its targets and to control its laser-guided missiles. Mounted in a rotating turret capable of swiveling in a 120-degree horizontal arc, or traveling from between $+30$ degrees to $-60$ degrees in elevation, TADS was the sister system to the Apache's Pilot's Night Vision Sensor system, or PNVS. In tandem they gave the AH-64 an awesome range of employments, which included Hellfire missiles, FFAR rockets, and/or Chain Gun fire.

"Good deal," commented Thornton. They all ducked as the faint sound of the returning Hueys reached their ears, duck-walking down into the arroyo's shadows and hugging its sides as the faint sound of Vietnamese voices floated across the desert to them.

"Bad memories, eh, fellas?" Silver rolled his eyes upward, causing Rowe to chuckle at the man's sense of humor under fire. No one had asked the blood-splattered ranger about the condition of his uniform, which was starting to smell of drying body fluids. They could all guess how he'd come by his baptismal, since Alan had explained about the two Viets while they were dragging 'Mr. Lucky' back from where they'd found him.

"No shit, Sherlock," offered Bo. "Reminds me of when my team ran into a full battalion of these assholes. They spotted the point and we ended up running for near half a day. By nightfall we were pooped, the point running face-first into this huge column of granite stuck right out there in the middle of the fucking jungle.

"Well, we boosted each other atop that bastard, which was just big enough around for us to put in a wagon wheel. The first NVA scouts came snooping around about ten minutes later. We heard them right below us, then damn near shit our britches when they settled in for the night, bringing a fresh tracking unit up behind them.

"We froze our asses off, afraid to eat any speed but damn near too tired to stay awake. The NVA stayed until early morning, shoving off just before daylight. I called in a bunch of fast movers who ripped the jungle wide open all around us. They musta killed one helluva lot of Chucks that morning, at least the body parts that rained down outta the sky made it seem that way.

"After the air strike, we called for extraction. A Jolly Green came in and lifted our shakin' hips right off the rock we'd clung to all night. Needed Cobras to run interference for us, and they did a fine job of it, too. One PJ got greased, but we got the body out. No hits on my team, but we stood down for damn near two weeks afterward."

Everyone was silent for a moment, their thoughts taking them to other places in other times. Finally, as the roar of three choppers in trail washed over them, Frank broke their solemnness. "Yeah, fellas, those were the good old days, weren't they?"

Their laughter was drowned out as Phong's air force landed, troop bays quickly filling with both the living and dead. In under two minutes, they were airborne once again, leaving behind a blood-soaked battlefield and nearly fifty of Canales's finest guns-for-hire rotting in the sun. Calvin spoke rapidly into his radio's handset, advising the Apache that their pigeons were at altitude. He nodded his head several times, ending the conversation with an excited "Roger, out!" Looking at his friends, he couldn't keep the excitement out of his voice as he told them the gunship was making its final lineup on the three sitting ducks.

Payback was a motherfucker.

# CHAPTER

## 12

Bailey rolled over in the surplus cot provided as a bed for the exhausted agent upon the team's return to the DEA launch site. Although asleep, he was aware that the dream was beginning again, the first few frames flickering across his mind's eye in slow motion as his subconscious kicked into gear. It was as if he was standing outside of his physical being, watching himself sleeping, seeing the first few beads of sweat beginning to form on his brow despite the air conditioner's hum in the background. Then he was sucked back into the netherworld of his inner memories, reality replaced by the vividness of his own experience.

The *cabo* slid down on one knee, his left hand half-raised as the right remained gripped tightly around the pistol grip of his M16. Bailey, the third man in the their ranger file, followed the point man's example, turning ever so slightly to their right flank so he could provide cover fire if necessary. He knew Roberto, the Sal M203 gunner, would be watching the left flank as the team alternated their rifle barrels down the line. It was quiet except for those noises that they needed or wanted to hear around them. If the point man was signaling a halt, it meant he'd suspected or seen something out of the ordinary.

Peering into the thick scrub surrounding them, Bailey went over how he'd ended up snaking along a well-worn trail in El Salvador with a bunch of the meanest naval commandos he'd ever run into. As a SEAL assigned to the MilGrp, it was his job to do everything possible to train an effective waterborne strike force for the Salvadoran navy. His team had been in country for nearly six months, taking over the recon project from an East Coast team that had laid the groundwork. The Army's Special Forces had proved that the Salvadorans could effectively mount good reconnaissance when they trained and fielded the PRAL, a company based upon Vietnam's SOG projects. Now the Navy was being asked to do the same.

Calvin knew he wasn't supposed to be on the ground with this or any other indig team. Participation in combat was prohibited, as if the entire war wasn't in itself one huge operation that an advisor stepped into as soon as the C-130's wheels touched down on the hot tarmac of Ilopango Military Airport. The Congress apparently hadn't understood the definition of ''guerrilla warfare'' when they decreed American soldiers could only carry ancient Colt .45s with two extra magazines apiece, as if a Beret or SEAL could do a hell of a lot of damage with a handgun against an M16-armed fighter for the FMLN. Of course that restriction was modified after the ''G''s killed Al that night in the capital, spraying his body with 9mm rounds pumped out of a MAC-10 submachine gun.

Somebody who hadn't had to stuff the dead SEAL's bullet-ridden corpse into a slick body bag decided that the "trainers," as they were called, could now carry *defensive* weaponry like MP5 subguns or the much more effective Colt Commando, which Bailey still thought of as a CAR-15. Calvin remembered chuckling about the definition the embassy had provided of what an offensive weapon was as opposed to a defensive side arm. "Ya gotta understand," said the Marine armorer charged with distributing the new guns, ". . . a full-sized M16 is an *offensive* rifle 'cause it's bigger lengthwise. Now the Commando has a shorter barrel, carbine-style, so it's meant purely for *defensive* carry. Ya unnerstand now?"

Bailey understood. It was word games, BS, hocus-pocus, fucking magic. The politicians had just needed a body count before they felt bad enough to finally admit there was a war going on in Central America. Now they could pat each other on the back and decry the senseless act of the guerrillas that had forced the Congress to arm its military representatives in a fashion to give them a fighting chance if taken under fire. Still they had to play word games, dreaming up a category of firearms that probably had old Sam Colt spinning in his coffin. Calvin had checked out his six magazines and their contents, slamming an already loaded one into the rifle's well from his pocket. They'd had M16s since taking over the SEAL barracks in La Union, as well as Claymores, hand grenades, and stubby little M79s. The Congress had filled one body bag already; they'd have to wait a little while for another one to come along so easily.

The wry Salvo corporal looked back, holding up four fingers then pointing forward again. Bailey shook his head in acknowledgment. Four bad guys just up front. The team's mission was open-ended, meaning they could recon or ambush, depending on what targets presented themselves. Four guerrillas would be just about right for a team their size. Might even get a POW out of the deal if they worked it right. Bailey carefully worked himself forward, crawling past the compass man, who was busily doing a map check. Reaching the battle-savvy trooper, Calvin raised his head high enough to see where the four "G"s were located, confirming the corporal's observations and count for himself.

"Mi sergento, do we count them and move on, or . . . ?"

Bailey, sweat rolling down his face from the heat and excitement of the moment, shook his head in the negative. They'd been dropped off by speedboat three hours ago and ordered to work their way onto the base of the volcano, which was home to at least three hundred reported guerrillas. Two other "shark" teams had infiltrated by sea after theirs, each with a different mission. Bailey's people were the wild card, able to make contact or avoid it as they desired. Calvin wanted a POW. "Let's see if we can't grab us a *pollo*, eh? Major Hernandez might like a live chicken to talk to about what the hell's going on up here."

The point man nodded vigorously. A prisoner would earn them much respect among the other sharks, as the navy's recon specialists were known to their peers. "*Los otros?*" he asked.

"The others will die," replied Bailey. "We can't leave them around to tell their comrades about us. There's the other teams to think about, and our own safety getting out of here."

The soldier nodded in agreement. The gringo made sense. The corporal had been fighting the FMLN for three years, and he was pleased to have been given an American who was willing to do more than just sit and tell war stories. It was one thing to teach the skills of ambushing and raiding behind the safety of a compound's wire, another to go out the gate with one's students to see how good the classes had been. This gringo's credibility was proven by his courage in joining the team on a mission. Credibility and courage were important to the Latin frame of mind. "I will take us forward. We will take them quietly, with our knives. You and I will capture the prisoner; we'll pick him when we're closer. It is a good plan?"

Calvin had heard worse. He remembered whipping similar op orders out his ass during his own training exercises. Stuff that wouldn't have flown two feet in the tactics classroom at Coronado. Field expedient, that's how it often went. They'd done it all the time as kids playing at war; now it was for all the marbles in a place where the dead didn't come back to life. "Let's do it!" he ordered.

The fight was brief yet horribly ferocious. The guerrillas had only been half-surprised, with two more men there than were first expected. The two forces had gone hand-to-hand, kicking and clawing at each other in a frenzy of fraternal hatred. Calvin buried his issue K-Bar in a guerrilla's throat, ripping it out in a fountain of rich blood spray that coated the naval commando from head to toe. The Sal corporal succeeded in knocking one of the FMLN fighters senseless, dragging the man into the woodline as the others continued to struggle. Bailey watched as one of the sharks got his head caved in with a wooden rifle butt, brains splattering everywhere. When it was over, they were able to account for all the guerrillas, adding one of their own to the pile. The war-tough *cabo* ordered their fallen comrade's body cached under a heavy deadfall, his equipment distributed among the survivors. The POW was tied and gagged, his limp body slung beneath a sturdy length of sapling carried by two stalwart sharks. Bailey contacted their extraction team, and within four hours they were once again waterborne and headed for the safety of the naval base.

It had been one hell of a drunk that night, as Calvin recalled.


"Cal . . . hey, Cal! Wake up, man!"

Bailey opened his eyes, grabbing hold of Thornton's arm as Bo stopped rocking him back and forth. "What the hell? What's up? We gotta move . . . What's going on?"

Bo smiled at his friend's confusion. He'd awakened to the sound of Bailey mumbling in his sleep, then watched as Calvin slipped deeper and deeper into what was obviously not a particularly good dream. "You were rockin' and rollin' in your sleep, partner. Thought I'd get you up before you fell outta the damn bunk. You okay?"

The narc rubbed his face in both hands, swinging his legs over the end of the cot and groping for a cigarette from the open pack on the hardwood table next to him. Lighting it, he stood, grabbing at a camouflage Gortex Windbreaker hanging from a peg on the wall. "Gotta get some air, that's all. Must still be wound tight from the snatch."

Thornton followed his friend outside, shrugging into his own jacket as they passed by his bunk. The sky above was speckled with stars, a faint chill breeze coming off the low mountains that surrounded the small base built by the DEA to house its strike elements when they were called upon to operate along the border. Bo tagged along behind the narc, fingering the pack of butts he'd nabbed from Bailey's cot before they'd left the barracks. A few minutes later both men reached the perimeter's wire, a triple strand of concertina faced off by a border of cyclone fencing twelve feet high.

"I'm okay," rasped Bailey. "You can get back to sleep."

Bo laughed softly into the night. "Couldn't do that now if I was tired," he said. "You want to talk about it, I'm all ears. Sometimes it helps, sometimes it doesn't. Never know unless you try."

"What'd you think about El Sal, Bo? I mean, do you ever wonder about what it was we were doing down there?"

Thornton shrugged, zipping the Windbreaker tighter as the evening's coolness sought to invade it. "It was a half-assed war, and we were fighting it in a half-assed way. The Congress was so worried about Americans dying in a Third World country that they tried to ensure only the indig would bite the bullets. I think everyone who pulled a tour in country did a hell of a job, given the constraints and stupidity of how it was handled."

"Wasn't like Vietnam though, was it?"

"No. But then, nothing has been or ever will be like the 'Nam."

Bailey drew in a deep drag of smoke, then tossed the cigarette over the wire. "EL Sal was my war, Bo. I worked my ass off to get a slot on a team headed down-range, and I made it. We were a lot more low profile than you Green Beanies were, which was cool 'cause you guys took the heat off what we were trying to do down around the coast.

"After a while, after I started figuring out that no one was going to admit to anything we were being told to do, the damn war became a personal crusade for me. Shit, the Navy didn't want to know what we did, the country didn't want to know, our own damned government was playing hide-and-seek with itself when they handed out six thousand medals for those dudes who went to Grenada for three days while we'd been running shit for three months down along the Gulf! You think anybody—us, your people—are gonna get a combat patch or badge outta the shit we saw? Fucking-A no, my man, fucking-A no way.''

Thornton shook a smoke free from the pack in Cal's pocket, handing it to Bailey, who lit up without a word. Pausing a moment, Bo slipped another from the pack and lit it with Bailey's, which was already burning furiously. For a few moments the two stood and watched the stars chase each other, the sounds of the desert washing over them like a lazy tide.

''Thought you'd quit these things,'' observed Calvin.

''First one in a long time, Cal. My last good smoke came courtesy of General Gaston after he'd landed to yank Dave and me off the ground in Honduras. Gaston packs a mean cigar: you ought to try one some time.''

''Thanks but no thanks. Cigars rip me up too much. Bad enough I gotta be crapped out on Marlboros.'' They both laughed, flicking ashes at each other.

''You musta been dreaming about something you did or saw Down South,'' offered Bo.

''Yeah,'' replied Bailey, ''a shark recon team I straphung a mission with in La Union. POW snatch, some pretty hairy hand-to-hand to pull it off. Lost a damn good man in the process, then lost a full fucking team a week later on a bad insert. We never should have sent those boys in, and we damn well knew it! But the frigging headshed in San Sal wanted some solid poop on ''G'' activity farther south, and we'd pulled off some real beasties, so . . ."

"So everyone started thinking they were bullet-proof, and the bad guys proved you wrong, is that it?"

Bailey pushed his hands into his pockets, the cigarette hanging from his lower lip in resignation. "That's it. They whacked the team so fast there was no time to air-insert a rescue element. All we found were the bodies, badly cut up and all their gear gone. I knew everyone on that team, every swinging Richard. If the war wasn't America's, and it wasn't the Salvadorans', it damn sure became mine, and that's how I fought it, until they pulled us out for the last time."

"I heard about that project while I was up at the commando school in San Francisco Gotera. You guys did a hell of a job. The naval recon teams were every bit as gung ho as you bastards."

Bailey smiled at the memory of it all. There was a supreme sense of satisfaction in taking a hodgepodge of renegades like those sent to the Navy and turning them into a proud, capable combat unit. You worked your ass off, sweated your nuts blue, ate when you could, and slept the same way. Pretty soon you were talking Spanish like a native, and your thought patterns were adapting so you began thinking like the people you were charged with training and sometimes leading. You watched your people grow, saw them catch on, cheered them when they hit the bull's eye, and raised hell when they didn't. When the missions came up, you watched them launch, their faces aglow as they lifted off the deck or blew out to sea, their damned hands waving at you because some fucked-up, chicken-assed, bullshit artist in Washington didn't have a nut sack big enough to let you go with your kids when they needed you the most.

What killed you was when they killed them. When the bodies came back wrapped up in a shredded poncho, arms and lower legs flopping around as the dead men's friends grimly lifted them off the blood-splattered decking of a shot-to-hell Huey. You'd run up to help, half-afraid they'd push you away because you hadn't been there when the shit hit the fan and therefore hadn't earned the right to share in their grief and rage.

But they never did. Instead they'd make a hole for you to get in there and lift with them. Together you'd carry your friend over to the shed where the bodies were ID'd and cleaned up. The local mortician would come by later to groom the corpse, tucking it into a wooden coffin provided by the military. In the meantime the team would be cleaning its gear, and you'd be there with them, lending a helping hand and all the while wanting to know what the fuck had gone wrong. But you couldn't ask, because you hadn't been there; if you had been, you'd know. So all that was left to you was to wait until they wanted to talk about it, if they ever did.

It was because of this that Calvin began going on missions. It wasn't because he wanted combat; it wasn't because he thought it the macho thing to do. He just couldn't stand seeing the anger in his men's eyes every time they came home shot up and found him standing on the dock, his uniform clean and pressed, his pistol unfired and hung on a parade-ground pistol belt. They were fighting for him, fighting for his country's interests, and by God, they weren't going to go on taking all the chances just because somebody back home had a case of post-Vietnam guilt.

After all, what could they do to him? Send him back to San Diego and tell him to keep his mouth shut? That was when the war became his, when he realized he had to fight it alone or lose both his self-respect and the respect he had for his country.

"Yeah, they were some hardcore shakers and movers," replied Calvin to his friend's compliment. "After a time, we managed to get the system working and our losses stayed low. It was the best duty I had in the Navy. I'm still welcome in La Oooh, courtesy of the base commander himself."

"But the dreams don't quit, do they?" ventured Thornton.

Looking into the retired veteran's face, Calvin grinned. "Nope. Every once in a while something I do, or say, or smell even, kicks a switch over, and I'm back on the ground again. It's normal shit from what I've read. People coming out of especially intense periods of their lives often exhibit a desire to deal with them through dreaming. Most of the time I just wake up missing those dumb bastards who've run through my mind, wishing they weren't dead or so far away I can't call and ask how they're doing."

"That's how Frank feels about Korea, kid. For what it's worth, it's the same for me when it comes to Vietnam. Dirty little wars in dirty little places, that's what we get to fight. Our dads and grandpas got dealt a good hand when the enemy was so obviously putrid there was no question as to what a soldier's duty was. These days, shit. There's a lot of guys out there who'll never get to join the fucking VFW because their wars never took place. It's gotta be a heartbreaker."

Bailey snubbed the second cigarette out beneath his unlaced boot. "Fuck it, it don't mean nothin'. We gotta damn good war on our hands now, and today we pulled off one ace-high impressive score. I figure old General Phong is plenty pissed about losing those birds this afternoon, and whatever we get from our POW will help sink his scow permanently.''

Thornton punched the younger man hard in the shoulder, then wrapped a big arm around him, and together they began walking back to their hooch. ''You're wrong about it not meaning anything, Cal,'' he said as they sauntered across the small parade ground under the watchful eye of a tower guard. ''It means everything in the world to you, and that's enough. We gotta live with ourselves, kid. Duty, honor, country, those are great recruiting lines. In the end, though, you gotta be able to look yourself in the mirror and know you did the best job you could.''

Somewhere out in the desert's depths a coyote was calling, the sound a plaintive cry for attention in a land devoid of God's regard. Bailey had no problem getting back to sleep, leaving Thornton alone to write a letter to Linda, who was waiting patiently for her man in a house they'd built by the sea.

# CHAPTER

# 13

The eyes in Phong's head looked as if they were ready
to burst free of their sockets, so intense was the man's
fury at what he'd just been told. Thick, red veins appeared like highways across the expanse of his cheeks,
a heavy throbbing clearly visible along the general's jug-
ular as massive amounts of blood were pumped to the
Viet's shocked brain. All three helicopters shot down?
All of his hand-picked men burned to a crisp within thirty
seconds? It was too much to accept when just a half hour
before he'd been given a communiqué from the ground
commander saying they'd enjoyed an overwhelming victory over Canales.

The three men in Phong's office sat mute in the glow
of his rising anger. They knew this disaster had cost them
dearly in both machinery and manpower. The lack of
airmobile transport would mean an immediate cessation
of their long-range assaults over the Mexican border as

well as those of Arizona, Southern California, and Texas. In addition it would be extremely difficult to replace the Hueys, and costly. The gunmen were equally valuable to the organization, and their deaths put a serious crimp in Phong's ability not only to strike outward, but to defend himself against his enemies. Each of the three waited patiently if not in fear for Phong to grasp his senses, a challenge the man was obviously in a battle to meet.

Slowly the Viet managed to calm himself, finally sitting in the comfortable leather chair behind his desk and looking directly into each man's eyes as he began speaking. They were transfixed, like deer caught in the headlights of an oncoming car. There was no escape from the general's scrutiny, no excuse for additional failure. "We have been dealt a near-crippling blow," he said quietly, although it seemed to his hushed audience as if he were shouting. "Why the DEA would happen to have one of their gunships in the area I do not know. Our intelligence people must discover if it was just happenstance, or if there is a leak among us."

Upon hearing Phong's suggested accusation of a traitor in their midst, all three advisors glowered at each other. "If there is such a person among us, General, we shall find him!" exclaimed one brave soul. Phong shook his head in agreement and acknowledgment. He would personally shoot the man or woman guilty of betraying him—it was a promise made silently to himself even as the others jabbered away between each other.

"Silence!" he yelled above the din. When it was so, Phong once again spoke. "No plan is perfect and ours proves this. Yes, we have hurt Canales and we have sent a strong message to him that to oppose us means death.

He will hear of his losses soon, if the Mexican isn't already aware of them by now.

"But we, too, have suffered casualties. I must call this a draw between us, with the DEA the winner, as now they have all the right cards in their hands. Canales will know we are as vulnerable as he is, more so because this country's government is not as accommodating to its outlaw elements as is its Mexican counterpart."

"What happens next, Phong? Surely we will cancel our upcoming operations until the strike units are rebuilt and we again have air support." The speaker was Diem, fresh from his vacation in Florida and still slightly hung over from a surprise celebration thrown for the hit team the night before.

Phong pulled a yellow legal pad to him and made notes as he spoke. The others quickly opened their own notebooks, scribbling cryptic reminders of what the general was proposing. The scene reminded the aging warlord of better days, when the enemy was either VC or NVA. These days, he seemed to be everyone, and the thought was depressing. "Truly we are forced to cancel the next month's cross-border raids on our competition," Phong said. "Expect an inquiry from the government as to why helicopters registered to Phong International were shot down, and why they were apparently carrying armed men. We must prepare a cover story that the federal people will have to either believe or disprove—that is the S-2's challenge.

"Canales will not suffer the problems we can expect. The Americans will require action of the Mexican government, and they will promise an investigation which will never take place. With the current economic and political profiles, the United States can ill afford to push their southern neighbor too far. They can ask for assistance, but never will they be able to demand it.

"So, we can expect the bastard to continue and perhaps increase his caravans immediately now that he knows of our loss and therefore inability to engage him."

"Is there any way we can pull the man's beard, General?" The speaker known as Trang was Phong's S-2, a younger man than any in the room, but adept at this job.

Phong glowered at the man, his irritation stemming from the knowledge that his hands were now tied when it came to dealing with any of his Latin foes. The hit on the Colombian would receive even greater attention now that the combined slaughter in the desert was known. The DEA as well as other federal agencies would be swarming all over the Southwest, digging like excited rodents into anything that might provide a foothold for a case against Phong and his empire. Canales would be sitting on a beach somewhere with a drink in his hand, laughing at the Viet's predicament as he continued business as usual from his side of the border. "No! There is nothing we can do except protect what we have left and hope no direct evidence can be found to link me with what has taken place. Everyone is to conduct himself as a model citizen, that means no weapons in our homes, or carried on our persons. We shall become the grateful immigrants we're supposed to be, at a loss as to why this has taken place and who might be involved. It is a time for defensive moves, a subtle retreat until an attack can again be launched in safety."

With a wave, Phong dismissed them. When the heavy door to his office closed, the Vietnamese shook his head in frustration. Who could have predicted the DEA chopper being in the same area? They normally patrolled farther south. But, of course, recent activities could have influenced a change of operational areas on the government's part. His pilots never had a chance against the awesome power of the Apache, whose TADS system must have locked all three birds into the ship's computer-controlled guns within seconds.

Now that the government was permitted to shoot down aircraft suspected of smuggling drugs, it was no longer a game to trifle with the airborne resources of Customs and the DEA. Pilots were leery of becoming involved in the aerial transport of dope cargos, demanding huge payments up front for their efforts. On the other side of the house, the informants were making a killing, trading information, on air routes and personnel normally used by the drug lords, to federal task forces for the incredible bounties being paid. Business was becoming tougher and tougher to carry out, with the penalties for failure at an all-time high.

With a shrug, the general reached for his hand-fashioned pipe, lighting and sucking deeply as sweet-smelling smoke rose from the bowl. Phong needed to relax, to think and plan his next moves. It wasn't good for him to get this upset. After all, he wasn't getting any younger.

# CHAPTER

## 14

"So how we gonna do it?" Frank Hartung dug his teeth into a thick ham sandwich, tearing off an impressive hunk and chewing thoughtfully as he waited for Thornton to respond. They'd been at it all morning, working out plan after plan to get both Phong and Canales together on the U.S. side of the border. Bailey ordered a telephonic link established with Conrad Billings, his DEA control in Washington, D.C., but that normally productive well had proved dry, too.

"I dunno, Frank. We can't extradite Canales, because there's no proof of his involvement, and the Mexican government will drag its collective heels anyway. Phong owns a battery of lawyers who've thrown up a ring of legal steel around the man since your boys attempted to see him about the choppers registered to his company. There's no doubt the Mexican will continue to run his end of things from where he is, but Phong will have to

145

go underground for a while until the heat dies down.''

Alan Rowe leaned back in his folding chair, adjusting his Glock's shoulder holster so it rode a little more comfortably next to his muscular frame. ''Well, boys, unless we come up with something devious and downright shitty, our two redheaded stepchildren are gonna walk. All we've got for our efforts so far is one dead Colombian, half a hundred dead folks from all races, and four burned-out aircraft. Our POW spilled his guts about the hit in Florida and on Canales's people, but that'll all be flushed if it ever goes to court.''

''Court? Shit, you can forget our little songbird spending one second in a courtroom, given how we got hold of his sorry ass.'' Jason Silver drew the freshly cleaned and oiled *khukuri* across the back of his forearm, checking its keen edge as hair literally popped off with the swath.

''How about a sting operation?'' offered Bailey. ''You know, give each of the assholes something so big they've got to take extraordinary measures to get their grubby little mitts on it.''

Everyone in the room looked at the narc, whose eyes possessed a gleam of evil intent none of them could miss. ''Press on, McDuff. What's cooking inside that noggin of yours?'' urged Hartung.

''Well,'' began Bailey, ''we know Canales is the overall winner in this round between him and the general. Phong's gonna be up to his asshole in alligators while the Mexican sits back and regroups, which will mean he'll be looking to move some major dope into the country to make up for his recent losses.

''Phong's pissed, right? But he's gotta be cool, very low profile. But, what if he's given a chance to not only whip a big one on a Canales caravan, but given a chance to whack the man himself?''

Thornton snorted. "You mean like killing two birds with one stone?"

"Yeah, exactly!" replied Bailey. "We approach the Mexican on his side of the border and make a buy, something really major which he simply can't turn down. Our only stipulation is that Canales be at the transfer point if he wants the cash. We're some heavy folks in our own right, and we've heard how many loads he's lost, so we're looking for some reassurance he can get this one through.

"If he bites, we use Frank's PRU connection to leak word about the caravan to Phong's people. The general can't pass up an opportunity to take part in greasing the guy whose guts he hates the most right now and . . .''

". . . and we'll be there waiting, ready to rock and roll 'em all!" finished Silver with a huge grin of understanding plastered across his face.

"Airborne and Amen," added Frank. "We'll need some serious money, though, really impressive cash to make the kind of buy Canales would cross the border for."

Calvin poked a finger in the air, the smoke from his cigarette curling up around it as he blew a double lungful upward toward the ceiling. "Conrad can get us the cash; it'll have to be at least half the total purchase 'cause they'll want that up front. The trick'll be getting to Canales, making the deal, then getting home again in one piece."

Hartung raised a weather-beaten hand. "Me and the squid'll go. I know Mexico City like the back of my hand, and we both talk the lingo. Cal here raps that drug shit like the pro he is. I can pass my ass off as his personal bullet launcher.''

Everyone looked around the table, waiting for Thornton to give the plan his blessing. It sounded like the only way to roll the two master criminals together on the right side of the border, but Bo would be the one who decided whether it was worth a shot or not. ''Cal,'' he began, ''this sounds good, but it's got to be understood that we will be terminating the two primary targets. Especially Canales. That puke is mine no matter what happens to the Viet.''

Bailey nodded once. He hadn't forgotten Thornton's condition as laid out in Los Angeles. The Mexican's ass belonged to Bo, lock, stock, and barrel. ''He's yours, Bo. Billings already knows that, and the sanction is explicit with respect to Phong also. We can't allow a former Vietnamese general to go on trial for drug smuggling in this country. His testimony could hurt us with respect to certain activities he was privy to during the war, and it would cast needless embarrassment on the Vietnamese community as a whole. Phong gets a thumbs-down from the Administration, period.''

''Fine!'' exclaimed Bo as he stood. ''Cal, you get on the horn and handle setting up this high-speed dope deal. That's your bag, so I'll trust you to put together something Mr. Canales will want to hear about.

''In the meantime the rest of us are gonna go outside and get a little lesson from our own Long John Silver here about that blade of his. I called a friend of mine in Georgia, and he's shipping out enough *khukuri*s for all of us to take on our next launch. That's one bad-ass knife, especially after what I saw it do to that Viet of Jay's in the arroyo. We're gonna ditch these standard pieces for what the Gurkha lads like to carry, but I want

Jay to fill us in on how the damn thing works beforehand.''

The team rose as one, with Silver leading the men out into a shaded area used by the base's permanent party personnel as a kind of miniature park. They all took seats in the thick green grass, forming a circle around Jason, who had the Hartsfield *khukuri* in his hand, its sheath attached to his pants belt. The big knife gleamed in the former ranger's hand, the massive blade bent forward at an angle designed to deliver the maximum in chopping and cutting power. Only the sound of the wind as it blew through the compound was present as Jason began. ''What we have here is one mean mo-fo of a knife, gentlemen. The *khukuri* dates back to the 1600s, although the basic design is grounded in such sword forms as the Greek *kopis* and Iberian *falcata*. Despite its historical beginnings as a sword, the *khukuri* is very much a utility knife as well as a close-combat blade.

''In researching the blade, I've found there are two basic *khukuri* forms. The first has a blade whose back displays a full continuous curve from the handle out to the tip, kinda like a half-moon looks. The other group uses a blade which is sharply angled at one point along the back, so the blade dips downward to create a belly-first kind of look. There's not much advantage of one over the other, so don't dwell on it as we go along.

''Now, Phill, he prefers the first blade style except he's modified it by grinding a secondary cutting edge along the top of the blade, as you can see. That's so you can use his *khukuri* in a back stroke, which is cool except you lose some of the utility applications of the blade because you can't hold onto the back of this *khukuri* if you want to use it as a draw knife. The ones Bo's got coming are military issue *khukuri*s, which are traditional in design and workmanship.''

Rowe raised his hand with a question. ''Jay, why the little notch at the base of the blade?''

Silver laughed. ''Good question, Al. This here notch is supposed to represent a buncha things. The more fanciful among us have proposed it's there to catch an opponent's blade so you can snap it out of his hand. Looking at it, you can see there's just no way it'll do that, 'cause the geometry is all wrong. Other folks say it's shaped like the clitoris of Kali, a Hindu goddess. A better story is that the *triskul*, which is the name of this here notch, represents the trident carried by Shiva, the God of Destruction and War. Myself, I kinda like that one best of all. Most often, though, the notch is used to either pull nails or can be modified to keep the blade inside its sheath on a peg arrangement.

''Now the Gurkhas toted these things into battle against the British, and they plain scared the hell out of them. The *khukuri*'s secret is in its shape, which is such that maximum force is transferred at the point of impact. Just about anywhere you hit on a *khukuri* will deliver a serious-business blow, especially if you leave the hand open when drawing the knife rearward, controlling the blade with just your thumb and forefinger. As you bring your arm forward, you also whip the knife forward in your hand, closing the fist just as the blade strikes its target. The result is a complete transfer of the energy generated by both your arm and hand to the forward-weighted blade . . .''

''. . . which means heads are gonna roll when that baby lands!'' exclaimed Thornton.

''Exactly,'' finished Silver. ''Now, granted, you gotta practice the technique a bit before it feels natural. But once you've got it down, it's as habit forming as pullin' your pud. Now bladewise this here Hartsfield piece is Rockwelled up to 60 or 61. Phill uses A2 tool steel, and he's turning out state-of-the-art blades. The "kukes" you boys are getting are probably made outta medium-grade carbon steel and are hitting the Rc scale at between 48 to 52. Most *khukuri*s are made soft so they'll hold up under extreme use and weather considerations. Them winters in the Himalayas can turn a high-tempered blade stone-cold brittle in no time at all, so the lower tempering serves to protect what might be the Gurkha or Sherpa's only tool."

Hartung nodded in agreement. He'd served in Nepal for a short time as an exchange NCO with a Brit Gurkha company, and he'd worked some with that fierce warrior clan's legendary battle blade. "Jay," he broke in, "the best way to sharpen them bastards is with a diamond hone, although we'll probably have to put our issue 'kukes' on a grinder when they get here. They take a mean edge once you've got one going, and it'll hold up forever unless you start beating rocks or something like that with it. I'd dump the two little knives that come with the scabbard; hell, they're mostly for show anymore anyhow."

"Agreed!" replied Silver, who was not as surprised as much as he was impressed with Frank's knowledge about the *khukuri*. "What else you know about these, Sergeant Major?"

Hartung stood, wiping the back of his pants so loose blades of grass fell earthward. Stepping forward, he accepted Silver's knife, weighing the hefty blade in his hand as he began speaking. Thornton couldn't help but smile, thinking how it was too bad so many of the old ironclads like Frank were leaving the army. The new guys could learn a lot from vets like the sergeant major, who'd been with SF when it was hard. "I can't add much to what you've already told 'em, Jay, but I do know the Gurkhas swear by these here knives and have used them in battle more than any other so-called 'fightin' knife' in recent times.

"When I was humpin' a ruck in Nepal, I heard the boys telling stories about a Gurkha named Havildar Badar Singh. Now this trooper took on some thirty-five men, killing most of them with his *khukuri*. If you know your history, that makes our Jim Bowie look like some kinda punk, given he's only credited with maybe half that many himself. A lot of our own knifemakers look down on the *khukuri* 'cause they don't unnerstand how the knife works. It's a hell of a working tool in the right hands, and it can do just about anything you ask of it without falling apart. Me, I'll be peaches-and-plum happy to belt one of these sons of bitches on again."

After Frank handed Jason back the big Hartsfield design, they wandered outside the perimeter to a dump pile of old lumber, where Silver demonstrated different strokes and chops with the knife. Each man took a turn at cutting several lengths of pine in half, then practiced drawing the weapon from its scabbard. Everybody was impressed with the ancient battle blade, and Thornton was glad he had asked his friend to blue-label the package out to an address they were using in Taos. At the end of the session, Bo ordered each man to begin working with his *khukuri* as soon as they arrived, with Jason in charge of making sure the blades were properly sharpened. The big commando then dismissed them, as it was time for the evening meal, teaming up with Frank as the other SPRINGBLADERS dashed for the mess hall.

"So what's up, old man?" quizzed Hartung, aiming

a soft punch that landed against Bo's shoulder.

Bo shook his head from side to side, watching his team as they playfully pawed at each other before cascading into the DEA chow hall with all the courtesy of a Mongol horde. They were damn good men, he thought. Hard-living and hard-working men. Not a pansy or wimp among them. Not a cry baby or complainer in the group. At the same time, they were the most compassionate and thoughtful bunch of thugs he'd ever soldiered with. He'd seen them give everything they had in their pockets to a needy child or a war-weary mother whose language they couldn't even speak. They'd built shelters for the poor, bridges where there were none, hope where hope had long since vanished. Regardless of the color hat they'd worn while in uniform, they were cut from the same sturdy tree, and God, how he loved them. "Looka the animals, Frank. You'd thing they hadn't eaten in two weeks, the way they're tearin' into the chow line!"

Hartung laughed. "Yeah, they're crazy hungry all right. Hungry to get this damned mission finished so they can go back to their girlfriends and homes and live like human beings again. You gotta admit that spending yer afternoon whacking pine boards in preparation for human skulls isn't exactly a common pastime for most of us these days."

Thornton grunted in agreement. He'd mailed his letter off to Linda, who'd returned from Paris early. She'd dialed the number he'd left, connecting with Conrad Billings, who'd told her Bo was deployed. Billings said she'd taken it pretty well, but Bo knew the girl would be pissed. He knew she loved him, as he had finally admitted he did her. It had been a long letter. "Better their heads than ours. You think the squid and you can get into Mexico and out in one piece?"

Frank kicked at a stone in his path, sending it spinning out into the gathering gloom of the evening's approach. "Mexico's fucked these days, Bo. If Calvin can set up a meet with this Canales fellow right there at the airport so we don't have to go into the inner city, we'll be fine. If they know we're bringing a bag fulla cash in with us, shit, they could just rip us then and there, and no one would be the wiser. Whole damn social structure is flappin' in the wind anymore, makes ya feel sorry for the common man who hasn't got a say in anything."

"Yeah, well, life's a bitch. I'm concerned about you and the SEAL. If you don't like the setup, then we'll figure some other way to get our man across the line."

"Nawww, it'll go okay," responded Hartung. "The kid's come a long way since we did Tony Dancer. Cal will get us in and out no sweaty-dai! We offer to buy a big enough load, and Canales will turn sand to glass crossin' the border. We just go in hard and fast with nasty backgrounds all doctored up by Billings's people back east. Either the Mexican buys it or he doesn't, easy decision. I'm not worried; hell, we've gone into worse situations, haven't we?"

"Yeah, yeah, we have, you old tyrant. Let's get some food before the boys clean the place out." Putting his arm around his oldest friend, Thornton led them both into the loud confines of the mess hall. "Say," he added as they both grabbed silver trays from a stack by the door, "I didn't know you'd been to Nepal."

Hartung, ordering a double helping of mashed potatoes, smiled at the memory. "I ever tell you about a Sherpa girl I met on leave? Well, Sarge, unless you've ever done it on a yak blanket halfway up the side of Mt. Everest, you've no idea just how good a *good* woman can be!"

Behind them Rowe was just preparing to clobber Silver with a rock-hard bun in retaliation for the scoop of Jello the former recon ranger had slipped into his full glass of milk. What followed was a food fight that would have made Bluto proud, although the DEA base commander ensured the mess was cleaned up by Thornton's crew before lights out.

Some things never change.

# CHAPTER

## 15

*Somewhere in Burma . . .*

Bannion's eyes jerked open as the Huey pitched crazily on its starboard side, the sudden shift throwing a load of unsecured equipment out the open door. Clutching his rifle between his knees, the narc scooted up next to the ship's fire wall, warily watching the door gunners as they began blasting away at the thick jungle below. In an instant, one of the gunners began coming apart at the seams, green tracers ripping through his lower torso so that the flight deck was suddenly awash in spilled entrails.

The narc jammed his carbine beneath a stack of unused body bags, sliding on his hands and knees over to the destroyed form of the gunner. Pulling the bleeding corpse away from its canvas seat in the Huey's hellhole, he wedged himself behind the M60, grabbing the twin butterfly triggers and swinging the gun's barrel downward where it might find a target. The rancid smell of death was trapped in his nostrils despite the howl of the wind blowing through the injured airframe. A second flurry of firing caught the pilot unaware, and Bannion curled himself up as the aluminum floor below him came apart under the steady pounding of a hundred different bullets. It was as if they were trapped in a flying fishbowl with no place to go to escape the steel-and-copper hornets that sought them out. Mike saw the side of the copilot's flight helmet explode outward, a mass of slippery brain tissue following the fiberglass fragments. The Huey's nose dipped low, then dropped as the pilot took a round between the eyes. Bannion couldn't hear the crew chief, whose mouth was wide open in a combination of terror and professional concern as he yelled at Bannion to "hang on, 'cause we're going in!"

The Huey began to spiral downward, throwing men and equipment from its open doors, as no one had bothered to belt themselves in after leaving the raid site. Musta flown right over another fucking camp, Bannion thought and swore to himself as he gripped the gun mount. The jungle loomed closer as the ruptured airship rushed toward it, smoke trailing from the huge turbine engine and hot oil spilling from a hundred punctured feed lines. Mike's mind was working with the speed of two Crane main-frame computers. He knew he had his side arm and knife secured to his combat harness, which he was still wearing. He'd lose the rifle in the crash, there was no doubt about that, if it was still on the bird. If he survived the impact, he'd have to bust ass to get at least one hundred meters away from the Huey to avoid being burned alive or worse, captured. Thoughts of SERE school at Fort Bragg rose to the surface of his consciousness. Had Colonel Rowe thought these same thoughts when faced with the possibility of his own capture? Shit, Bannion reminded himself as the wounded bird's skids crashed through the first layer of trees, SERE's gonna look like a piece of cake if I make it through this!

It was like being pushed off a high dive blindfolded. Mike felt the Huey's tail boom hang up on something, then heard a gut-wrenching mechanical roar as the bolts holding it to the main cabin were torn free of their housings. He saw the ground exploding toward him at what seemed like the speed of sound, and without thinking, he swung himself back into the main troop bay just as a monstrous tree limb punctured the thin aluminum wall he'd been huddled against seconds before. The crew chief was gone. Mike grabbed for the back of the pilot's seat and managed to jam his upper body between the two dead men's chair backs just as the bludgeoned aircraft rammed into the ground. For a moment Bannion blacked out, the force of the impact knocking him senseless with its brutality. Inside the narc's brain a single signal was screaming for him to awaken. Survival! He rolled his head forward and gazed groggily around at the mayhem surrounding him. Shards of plexiglas had peppered him when the front windows were smashed inward, their fragments scattered about the jungle floor like thousands of imitation diamonds. Both pilots looked as if they'd been beaten to soggy pulps, their bodies formless inside the single-unit flight suits they wore. "Gotta get out . . . gotta move . . . now!" Bannion yelled at himself. He could smell J4 all around him, and the thought of burning to death in a pool of aircraft fuel brought added incentive to his efforts.

Bannion clambered out the starboard side of the smoking coffin, noting that the Huey had come to a rest at a crazy angle, its nose pointing downward yet kitty-corner

to the ground. He was deaf in one ear and felt several
sticky spots along his ribs where he'd been bounced like
a damned tennis ball between the two flight seats. Dropping to the matted earth, he fell into a crouch. Without
knowing it, he'd yanked his pistol from its holster, although he couldn't see a rifle of any kind anywhere near.
Except for the hissing of the broken bird's innards and
the smoke wafting skyward, the jungle was quiet.

"Okay you special forces bastards, here's Mike out
in the middle of shit's own homestead, and he knows
the bad guys are inbound with a vengeance. What was
the first priority in 'Save Your Ass 101'?'' Get away
from the wreck! Bannion scooted on his hands and knees
toward the tree line, which was only meters away from
where he'd landed. His had been the third Huey in trail
when they were hit; certainly the others had seen them
go down and would be coming back to extract any survivors. Cannon would know his One-Zero was aboard
number three, and Stan the Man wouldn't leave his boss's
ass hanging in the wind unless . . . unless they couldn't
get back in or wouldn't take the chance, not knowing if
there was anyone left alive.

Bannion rapidly ran a hand down the front of his combat harness. He was looking for a smoke grenade, any
color smoke would do, in order to signal the birds he
was alive. His harness was empty! Pen gun flare! Mike
ripped the OD nylon pouch open and jerked the black
firing device free, a red flare already screwed into its
mouth. Looking upward, he aimed at a hole in the jungle's roof, releasing the firing pin and watching as the
tiny rocket roared toward the small break in the foliage.
Without warning, it spun off to one side, bouncing off
a thick tree limb and shooting angrily downward, where
it buried itself in the thick, dead vegetation of the jungle's

floor. Bannion was about to retrieve a second flare when he heard the voices, voices that were too close for comfort.

Dropping onto the earth, he wiggled his way beneath a thick stand of hanging vines, pulling himself along with his hands and pushing with his booted feet. The voices were louder now, excited and questioning as the men to whom they belonged discovered the remains of the crashed chopper. Bannion spoke basic Burmese, and he understood most of what was being said. They were celebrating their victory, and hopeful of finding both booty and a survivor or two. Mike knew they had probably been shot down by either a band of renegades, guerrillas, or drug smugglers, the latter of which would be his worst nightmare. It was more than likely a patrol returning from a scouting mission that had fired on the Huey, a single M60 hitting the big time on a fluke flyover. Bannion didn't hear any other choppers in the air above him, meaning the lead pilot had ordered his crews to di-di for the base. They'd be back, but in force and with an extraction team to recover any survivors or bodies. Mike didn't blame the man; he'd have done the same under the circumstances.

"Well, old boy. All we gotta do is escape and evade these monkeys for the next few hours, and everything will be just all right," he told himself. Ensuring that his handgun was secured in its holster, Mike drew his Battle Zone from its sheath, tucking the huge blade up alongside his inner forearm so he could crawl without hanging the big knife up. By the sound of it, there were at least seven or eight people rampaging around the crash site, and a chance encounter would have to be silent on his part, or they'd be on top of him like a pack of dogs. He had water, a few candy bars, a compass, his pistol, and several extra magazines, as well as the knife. He'd have to find a place to hole up for a few minutes so he could check himself for any injuries he hadn't felt yet, but his first aid kit was intact on the pistol belt alongside his holster. The key to a successful E&E was to keep one's head and to be as prepared as possible equipment-wise. He'd learned that lesson well at Fort Bragg, coming out one of the only two men on his team to evade the SF instructors looking for them during the final phase of the course.

Now he was doing it for real with the stakes his life, his freedom, and maybe his sanity. A captured DEA agent would be worth ten times his weight in gold to the drug lords of Burma. Bannion had no doubt they'd keep him alive, at least for a while. That didn't mean it would be a pleasant existence, or even a semicomfortable one. The SLAM teams had put the big hurt on dope moving through the region, costing the smugglers millions of U.S. dollars and hundreds of men. Mike Bannion didn't want to meet his enemy face-to-face unless there was a smoking gun's barrel between them, and that item was sure to be missing if he was a POW.

Slowly, silently, the agent snaked his way deeper into the jungle. He would become a part of it until a rescue team got its act together and pulled his ashes out of the fire. Mike Bannion was a man on the run, with a whole country full of jungle to get lost in unless he fucked up and got his young ass captured.

Behind him the smugglers were happily mutilating the pilots' bodies, chattering at their success and admiring their newfound watches, rings, and keepsakes, ignorant of Bannion's presence only meters from where they sat. They would look for any others later; now was the time for looting and taking revenge on those who shot at them from the sky as they moved their lord's valuable cargo down from the mountains and into the cities, where it could be sent across the ocean to America and Europe. In their own minds and in their own way, payback was a motherfucker.

# CHAPTER

## 16

For the next four days, Thornton prowled the tiny encampment like a caged panther. Jason and the sergeant major flew out the morning after Silver's *khukuri* demonstration, destination Mexico City. Billings and Bailey had worked overtime, pulling in favors and demanding a few in order to make a connection with Canales. Entire agent and informant networks were put in jeopardy, but Billings's use of a presidential sanction overrode even the most strident objections. Calvin had confided to Bo his concerns about the DEA becoming a nightmare of career climbers and technocrats. The announced war on drugs had boosted the agency's status as a place to earn one's federal retirement, and the slugs were worming their way into the structure, burrowing their nests deep within the agency's guts, where all one had to do was play it nice and safe to succeed.

They'd sparked Canales with a five million-dollar offer. Half the cash in U.S. currency to be paid up front if the deal and its conditions were agreed to by the Mexican. The rest, again paid in full, delivered on the U.S. side of the border at a spot designated by the two "dope dealers," Silver and Hartung. Bailey had spun a convincing portfolio on each of the two SPRINGBLADERS, to include ongoing investigations and previous records and releases for a number of state and federal violations. The devious agent even hooked a known drug lawyer into backstopping his two newest "clients." A hefty stint in a federal prison was held over the attorney's head, for a number of IRS charges now on hold in exchange for the man's cooperation. Canales was impressed enough to schedule a meeting within twenty-four hours of their first call, the site to be at his home in Mexico.

Bo sprinted the last fifty meters of his workout, breaking down into a slow jog as he began a cooling-down period. Exercise was the only way he could burn off the tension of not knowing what was happening with his friends and comrades, so he rotated running with weight training and long hikes through the hills surrounding the MSS. After two more laps of the compound, he stopped to watch Rowe and Bailey as the two men practiced with their new *khukuri*s. They'd taken the knives over to the machine shop upon their arrival, grinding a working edge on each blade, then finishing it with a hand-held diamond hone. Silver DXed the leather scabbards, having pre-ordered some custom fittings from John Carver, which were overnighted to the team. "You can buy any number of *kopis*-style camp knives today," Jason had told them while they were carefully bringing their edges up to combat status, "but *khukuri*s like these have gone to war since the 1600s. I'd bet a dollar to a doughnut this knife has seen more actual hand-to-hand combat than anything else still around today, and it costs less than fifty bucks plus a few hours of elbow grease to own one. Battle-proven, that's a winning ticket any way you cut it in my book!''

Thornton began his stretching exercises as he watched the two compete against each other, seeing who could cut a two-by-four in half with the least number of strokes. They went on to split a number of overripe melons from the mess hall's refuse pile, finishing with some drawing exercises from the scabbard. Both wore their knives on the right side of their combat harnesses, the scabbard set up so the retaining strap could be popped free with the thumb, the *khukuri* slipped rearward and out. ''Works better this way than the traditional drawing upward and out,'' explained Rowe, ''and if you place the opening slot in the front, you take a chance of cutting the retainer, plus you're pulling the scabbard up and forward along with the knife, because the belly grabs the angle of the sheath as you withdraw it.'' Thornton agreed.

Linda had gotten a call through to Bo the evening before, thanks to Billings, who'd cleared her and given the worried girl the site's classified number. They'd talked freely for over an hour, Linda concerned with Bo's safety as well as with that of the rest of the team. ''Enough is enough, Bo,'' she'd told him. ''You've earned a heck of a lot of money from these things, but now they're calling anytime there's a situation they can't handle by any other means than blowing away 'the primary targets.' Let them change the laws if it's so damned tough to catch these bastards legally. You and the others are being turned into bounty hunters, and I don't think you ever intended it to go that route!''

Thornton wiped a palmful of sweat from his face, rubbing his hand dry against the soft fabric of his running shorts. She was right, of course; he hadn't meant to become a hired gunslinger for the government. As a matter of fact, the men he'd met over the course of his career who filled those shadowy slots had always irked him somewhat. He hadn't known of their official sanctions status, nor was he privy to their operational guidelines and controls. It was easy to be critical when you wore the uniform or a suit and tie, but the reality of the matter was that there seemed to be a place for everybody in the world of covert warfare.

"Mr. Thornton, hey, Mr. Thornton! I got some news for you!"

Bo turned as a clean-cut young man from the radio shack ran up, a FAX message in his hand. "What's the scoop, junior? Fan mail for me or what?"

The support agent smiled, his glasses slipping down onto his nose for just a moment while he busily scanned the message one final time. Satisfied, he handed the note to Thornton. "Make sure you burn it, Mr. Thornton. Or you can drop it back off with me and I'll take care of it for you. No copies, please." Then he was gone, walking rapidly back to his air-conditioned office.

Bo read the message, a grin breaking across his face as he did so. They'd done it! The two lunkheads were in Los Angeles and would be landing in Taos by late afternoon. Canales, code-named "Ajax," had confirmed the contract and would personally deliver it at the location specified. With a shout, he drew Rowe and Bailey's attention, waving the white slip of paper high above his head as they began loping toward him. "Hurry it up, meatballs!" he growled. "It's show time!"

# CHAPTER
## 17

Hartung slipped the phone back onto its cradle, then spun around in his chair so he could address everyone else in the room. "The fix is in, gents. Our man in Taos should be giving one of Phong's stooges a call right now, wanting to sell some hard information on a load coming across the border the day after tomorrow. The general will no doubt want a meeting with this 'informant,' but our lad's credentials are as solid as his loyalty to his new country. Once Phong hears Canales himself is to accompany the caravan, there's no way he'll be able to resist taking the man out himself."

"I can't figure out why the Mexican is going to do it. Sure, there's some serious money involved, but the risk is damned high."

Rowe nodded his understanding of Bailey's concern, then tossed his thoughts out for consideration. "Whatever we might think of Mr. Canales and his chosen profession, remember he is both a Latin and a man. His organization has been taking a beating for months now at the hands of Phong. The assassination of the Colombian was a slap in the face of all the Latin heads of the dope trade, again, at the hands of Phong. Canales makes a move to avenge himself and his comrades, only to have a planeload of his best gunmen wiped out before they can chamber a round. That's a lot of bullshit for a dude like the Mexican to take.''

"So you figure he's doing a 'Macho Comacho' kinda gig?'' asked Silver.

"Sure,'' replied Rowe. "Canales is supposed to control the border. It's up to him to find safe routes into the U.S. for shipments, regardless of what they are. He's on the edge now. His men are wondering if he's got what it takes to hold it together as a man they can follow, and his business associates are probably concerned about his reliability as well.''

"Five million ain't a bad incentive either!'' grumped Hartung. "You shoulda seen his eyes when we opened the bags with the cash. For a second or two I thought he'd take us out and keep the down payment for his time. But Old Man Greed stepped in and the rest is history.'' They all laughed at the sergeant major's description, each knowing full well how close their two friends had been to a violent, unsolved death.

"We gotta get moving then,'' broke in Thornton. "According to the setup, Canales will have to put together a mule train, outriders, security, and the dope itself within twenty-four hours. That's not gonna be as tough as it sounds, given all the shit these clowns have been stockpiling just across the border for over a year now. Bailey tells me there's caches of pot, coke, heroin, and a buncha other shit scattered all along our southern frontier. Movers like Canales simply pick and choose according to the deal at hand, and it's easier to stock the stuff than try and bring in individual contracts.

"At the same time we've given Phong damned little time to do more than react. He's gonna hate it, being the planner he is and the pressure his organization is under. Either he goes for the gusto and sends in the cavalry, or he allows Canales a victory which he's paid in blood to deny him. I'm willing to bet the Viet goes to guns. The bait's too big and the opportunity to finish the Mexican off is too tempting to pass up."

"So how's this little party going to go down?" asked Silver. "We can't hit both these geeks at once. We're good, but we're not that good."

Frank stood, wandering over to a map of the area designated by him and Jason as being where the final transfer of funds and drugs was to take place. It was wildly desolate country, devoid of any redeeming factors but one. It was a great place to kill a lot of people without attracting attention. Punching a hardened finger into a point on the map, Frank outlined their operations order. It took a half hour to go through, with few interruptions from those listening. Hartung had spent the last three days, while dealing with the Mexican, working out a feasible way of hitting both groups at the same time.

"So that's the sum of it, guys and gals. Our target priority has to be *only* General Phong. I know how Bo feels about the SF team Canales whacked, but the only way we can deal with him is to either let the Viet blow him away for us, or take him out as a target of opportunity." Frank tossed a stern look at Thornton, who merely nodded.

"Okay then," continued Bailey from where he sat. "You're recommending we get into position ASAP, but with the intent of gonging Phong when he makes his appearance. We let the general initiate whatever party he's got planned on the Mexican's troops, then step in when a shot presents itself and take Phong. What about the rest of the animals?''

"Like Frank says, Phong's the primary. We'll need to use support troops this time, the Apaches and perhaps a doubled-up team of SLAM personnel if Billings can wrangle a platoon free." Thornton slipped off the edge of the table he'd been sitting on, pulling his *khukuri* from its sheath and tracing a line from the proposed ambush site to where the reaction force could be placed on standby.

Calvin jotted a few lines in his notebook before answering Bo's question. Billings had told the agent they were stretching their resources badly on this one, the potential for compromise increasing with each out-of-agency request. A SLAM platoon was their only alternative when it came to giving the SPRINGBLADE team the backup it needed while maintaining any kind of dependable security within the sanction's parameters. Even so, the president would have to give his personal approval on this one. "There's a new platoon graduating in Virginia the end of next week. Mostly young studs coming over from the Forces. This would be a good 'training' exercise for them . . . and frankly, they're the only game in town.''

Frank Hartung looked over at Bo, who was studying the map. The room was silent, heavy with anticipation at what the team's One-Zero would have to say. The mission was getting hairier by the minute, and it would be Thornton who decided whether they would take it any farther. Aware of their attention, Bo spun around and faced the men, who were both his dearest friends and fiercest supporters. "We go," he announced. "Everyone

works all night on pre-mission prep. Frank coordinates.
Cal? You get that SLAM platoon in the air by midnight.
Full combat load. I want to see the platoon leader as
soon as they hit the ground running. We'll want two
Apaches as escorts, one loach for C&C, and three Hueys
or Blackhawks for transport in and out. In addition I
want a .300 Win-Mag from the inventory at Bragg. Five
rounds of that special stuff from DELTA goes with it.
Any problems?''

"Yeah," roared Frank as he broke the silence with a
sergeant major's baritone. "We're wastin' time bumpin'
fuckin' gums! Everyone get movin' and start bustin' ass.
I want Jason with me and Rowe with Calvin. Bo floats
and handles the air asset coordination. Get it on, men!
It's killin' time again!''

Gee, I love that kinda talk, thought Silver as he jogged
out the door after the cigar-puffing Korean vet. Jason's
train of thought was jolted back on track as Hartung began
issuing orders with the speed of a well-oiled German
MP-40, the former recon specialist scratching reminders
of his night's taskings on a well-worn legal pad he'd
pulled from his fatigue trouser cargo pocket.

It was time to rock 'n' roll.

# CHAPTER

## 18

"We must strike and do so at once! The fool leaves me no choice, no alternative. What possesses him to do such a thing now?" Phong stared at the men gathered on his porch, the hot New Mexican sun glaring down upon the group, which had been meeting since early morning. The news about a major shipment to be made within days had shocked the general to his core. The fact Canales would accompany it was simply mind-boggling to the Viet. The source of the information was impeccable, a former PRU scout who'd been living in Taos for several years and who was known for keeping his own counsel. The man's price was fair, a fact that gave him even more credibility in Phong's eyes.

"I do not like it," reasoned Diem. "The deal is too large, and it comes about as if by magic or design. It's as if someone wants to put both you and the Mexican side by side, a mountain of drugs the bait. I recommend caution, my general.'' Diem lit a cigarette, blowing the acrid smoke downwind.

Phong studied the faces of the men from whom he sought advice. They were trusted comrades, loyal only to him. But even he understood the impact of the disaster they'd suffered in the desert. His lawyers were working overtime to stall federal hounds demanding access to his records, their fees enormous as they dropped obstacle after obstacle across the pathways leading into Phong International. His own organization was still stunned from the manpower losses they'd taken. Diem's operation in Florida was forgotten in the light of an entire combat section being lost within seconds to the DEA's lone gunship. Whatever the Mexican had lost paled in comparison, as he was still free to operate, to make his money as well as to restore his position as a key figure in the trade. Now it was Phong who was under the gun, and the Viet didn't like the feeling one damn bit.

Clenching his fists, the general squeezed his eyes shut as he forced himself to stay rational. There truly was no option left to him but to confront the wily Canales. Yes, it was a foolhardy move on the Mexican drug lord's part, but one which was sure to pay extra dividends in terms of establishing himself as once again having the ''juice'' to make things happen. Five million dollars worth of contraband was serious money. Although Phong had never heard of the two men who'd swung the deal just days before in Mexico City, his intelligence on them showed they were major players. A successful take-down on his part would reap some badly needed cash, a massive stockpile of easily convertible dope, and a final chance to blow the cocky Mexican's head clean off. The stakes were high, yes. But Phong was a man used to high stakes and dangerous risks. If Canales wanted a confrontation,

Phong would give it to him in spades. The key lay in the Mexican's betting the Viet wouldn't have the guts to attempt an interdiction at this stage of the game. Phong opened his eyes and smiled.

Once again he was the tiger.

# CHAPTER

## 19

The heavily armed and burdened mule train slipped across the fenceless border just before dawn, only the dampened muffle of the animals' cloth-bound hooves disturbing the enforced silence of their guards. Well ahead of the caravan rode a contingent of seven especially alert riders, automatic rifles across their saddles, trigger fingers only millimeters away from dealing out magazines full of high-velocity death. In all, over forty hard men were riding for the Mexican this trip. He'd demanded only the most seasoned, the most trustworthy of his band of outlaws be involved. Canales himself rode center column, four bodyguards of his own choosing flanking their boss's every move, watching his every gesture, hearing his every command. In his own mind, the Mexican now knew how Villa had felt at the head of his legions so many years ago. *This* was power! It was all well and good to sit behind a stucco wall and issue directives, your body growing soft in the richness of the wealth the drug trade lavished on its practitioners. But to once again pick up a gun and face the devils themselves, that was a feeling Canales realized he had missed. Would Phong discover his bold move and react with a strike force of his own? It was doubtful. The Viet was being hammered for his stupidity of the last week; it was impossible for him to even leave his house without a horde of federal agents poking their noses up his ass. No, the good general had been defeated yet once more. Canales would deliver this, the largest shipment he'd attempted in six months, to the two gringos, and collect the remaining two-and-a-half million dollars they were to bring with them. He'd been pleased they'd checked out with his people in the intelligence section of the Mexican army; it was difficult knowing who to do business with these days, unless you owned a dependable information bank.

The Mexican was impressed with the Americans' selection of the route he'd been provided. He'd flown to the jump-off point by helicopter, two ancient C-47s making several trips apiece in order to get all the men, drugs, animals, and equipment in place. The crossing point itself was little used for this kind of thing; so completely desolate was it that most smugglers were content to keep it on file as a last-ditch alternative. The canyons and arroyos would allow maximum protection from discovery by air, a concern made even more important in light of the destruction wreaked on the Viet by the DEA's flying gun platform. Canales knew the dirt strip the two Americans wanted to use, although he was unsure how they planned to get the incredible tonnage he was bringing them out of it within a reasonable time.

But that was not his problem, he reminded himself. His problems were greater, more long-reaching in their effect upon his reputation and continued good business. The stupid Vietnamese had cost Canales millions, laying waste to what had been a profitable enterprise with few losses over the years. His business partners were more than just concerned at how he'd apparently lost control of their common interests, the death of the Colombian nearly toppling the Mexican from power. If he could pull this off, he'd be in a position to barter again, and the Viet would be humiliated on his home turf. They'd have to kill the man, of course. It would take a car bomb perhaps, or several independent teams of professional hit men. In any event and no matter what the means or cost, the general would be removed before the end of the month if Canales had any say in the matter at all.

Tugging the thick sheepskin coat around him, the drug baron glanced at his watch. It would be a long trip, he mused. They would reach the Americans around five that afternoon, atop a low plateau where the planes could get in and out despite the night's arrival. Canales would insist on the money immediately. The gringos could have the mules if they wanted them, or leave them to wander in the wilderness for all the Mexican cared. As soon as the money was in his hands, he'd be riding hard for the border. His scouts were mountain men, capable of guiding the main body out regardless of the night's blackness and uncertainty. By dawn, Canales would be back on his side of the border; he had a luncheon appointment in Mexico City, a date he intended to keep. In the meantime, though, he would enjoy this departure from his regular habits. The morning's sun was lofting over the mountaintops, a deep blush beginning to serrate the sky above him. The twin .44 Magnums in his belt felt good, their weight and power reassuring. It was a good day to be alive.

It was also a damned fine day to die.

# CHAPTER

## 20

Hartung swung the powerful Steiner field glasses back along the length of the plateau's lip, soundlessly counting the manned positions Phong's troop leaders had been emplacing since their arrival early that morning. SPRINGBLADE itself had been flown in a full eighteen hours before even the Viet's impressive airborne insertion, the team dropped off by a single Blackhawk, which hovered only long enough for the combat-laden men to leap from its skids before pulling pitch and heading back to the mission support site. Bo selected a rocky promontory from which to fight, each man given a sector of fire for which he was responsible. The night raider himself was lying quietly behind the butt of a hand-built .300 Winchester Magnum. A low base constructed from two ¾-filled sandbags acted as a burlap pillow for the heavy-barreled gun that SOCOM was currently fielding for especially important interdiction missions. Already locked into the weapon's breech was a specially designed round made on contract for the government. Purchased in lots of fifty, the bullet was the brainchild of a retired Army colonel who'd been involved in special operations as far back as the early fifties. An advisor to the CORDs program in Vietnam, the colonel began developing his own personal sniper program during that war, a war that saw long guns used far more than was normally acknowledged by any of the more popular military historians. The round the colonel was successful in developing was actually a highly sophisticated SABOT projectile, capable of tremendously flat trajectories and awesome transfusions of kinetic energy to the target area. It literally exploded soft tissue and bone upon impact, insuring one-shot kills at distances determined only by the quality of the selected delivery system and the accuracy of the shooter's eye.

Thornton was dressed in soft, loose-fitting fatigues. On his feet he wore lightweight, high-topped running shoes. His battle harness was curled neatly beside him, propped up by the *khukuri*'s sheath, which was attached to its right side. On his head he wore a freshly rumpled "boonie" hat drawn from the supply room at the MSS. His trigger hand was encased in a fingerless glove made from lambskin, the other free to adjust the $3 \times 9$ power scope fixed atop the rifle. Over his eyes he wore a pair of RayBan shooters glasses, their deeply tinted yellow lenses protecting his vision while cutting out the harsh glare of the desert sun. Bo had shaded the expensive optic to prevent it giving off a telltale glint, satisfied it was zeroed in for the master sniper after an hour on the range during their mission preparations.

Casing with the Steiners, Frank lay over on his side

and gulped a mouthful of water from his canteen. They'd strung camouflage netting over the stone enclosure, as protection against detection as well as exposure to the fiery sun above. Capping the OD plastic container, the sergeant major tallied up his figures in an open notebook, then spoke in Thornton's direction. "Thirty to forty of them down there from what I can see, well dug in and boo-coo automatic weapons. Several riflemen with scopes, probably to take out the burros on a first-priority basis. Haven't found the general yet, though."

Bo grunted, scooting himself closer to Hartung so they could speak easily. "Phong's been here before, other times and other places. He's not going to announce his presence until Canales shows, and even then I kinda expect it'll be a short-lived introduction on the Viet's part. The Mexican, on the other hand, shouldn't be too hard to spot. He's on a mission from God with this one, and you can bet he'll be showboatin' it for the benefit of his men and his 'buyers.'"

Bailey's voice reached the two men from where the narc was lying alongside a locked and loaded M60 LMG. "I radioed a description and direction of flight on those birds that brought Phong's army in. We'll nail that end of it down once the shootin' is over with, but I expect it's some independent act with a low threshold for where their money comes from."

Frank farted loudly, bringing a chuckle from the men around him. "Everybody's got to make a living. Old Phong musta come up with some big bucks to hire them choppers on such short notice. Good thing we unassed the MSS when we did—the general's moving fast ever since my man in Taos spilled the beans."

"No shit, Sherlock!" exclaimed Silver. The demo expert was manning a position that gave him an eagle's view down the canyon Canales would have to negotiate in order to reach the plateau. He'd ordered a second M60 for himself, wanting the heavy gun's range and penetration, given the terrain they would be fighting in. Atop the well-worn receiver, Jason had welded a heavy 4 × fixed scope, hoping to use it to search out targets once they went to ground. Like most gunners, Silver could fire the sixty in single-round shot groups when he wanted. It was an old skill he'd picked up on the ranges of Fort Benning, requiring only a light finger and a well-oiled trigger group.

Alan Rowe was manning their SAT-COM radio, an M21 sniper system tucked up beside him on a poncho liner. Rowe had twenty-five fully loaded magazines of Lake City match ammunition in his ruck, and a first generation ART scope with which to work. It would be his job to vector in the Apaches after Bo had confirmed a kill on Phong. After the war birds finished their job, which was to eradicate any signs of life within the target area Alan would designate, Rowe would then radio in the SLAM platoon, which was charged with mop-up operations, to include burying the dead under tons of rock blown from the canyon side. Billings had been quite clear about survivors from both sides. There wouldn't be any.

They were silent for a time, listening to the wind and watching the occasional lizard that scampered across the rocks. Silver saw a snake, its huge body zigging then zagging through the soft sand until it disappeared into a dark crevice. Above them a bird floated on the hot air currents generated by the depths of the canyon. It was a peaceful period for men who'd been working their buns off ever since Thornton's decision to continue the mission. "You're gonna whack Canales, aren't you?" Hartung was lying on his back, the camouflage netting splitting his face into a hundred different shadow lines as he enjoyed the afternoon's heat.

Beside him Thornton shrugged. "Yeah. Figure Phong will want to pull the trigger himself, so he's probably down there somewhere, laying up sorry with a long gun just like me. I'll need you to pinpoint him with the binos, then call it when you figure he's gonna do the dirty deed. Canales is mine. I owe it to that team his people wasted, and it'll be a good lesson for the general."

"Lesson?" questioned Frank.

"You can't always get what you want. General Duc Phong isn't going to enjoy the satisfaction of dumping the Mexican, I am. The Viet is going to get what he needs, though, and that's killing. His boys are gonna open up with everything they have when that first round goes off, and Phong won't be able to stop it. Soon as I terminate the Mexican, I'm putting the cross hairs on the general. You'll need to spot for me, Top."

Frank blew a quiet stream of pent-up breath out through their burlap roof. "No sweat, Sarge. Kinda thought a .300 was overdoing the shot we've got from here on Phong. But if you're shooting down that canyon at any range over five hundred meters, well, you'd need the extra punch."

Bo laughed quietly. "No one gets much past you, do they Frank?"

"Nawww," replied the thirty-year man, "I've seen so much shit in this lifetime, I don't think there's much more that can be dumped on the old sergeant major's plate. The countries change, the faces and the names. Sometimes the rules get a little twist to them; that just keeps things interesting. But, for the most part, it's the same old song and dance."

"Linda wants me to hang SPRINGBLADE up," suggested Thornton. "She's wanting me home and concerned it's getting too easy for the boys upstairs to use us."

"Girl's got a point, Bo. When we started this thing it was only supposed to be a one-shot deal. Then came Ricardo Montalvo, then Angel, then the Russian . . . shit. Now we're back to bumpin' off dopers our government shoulda been able to put on ice using the justice system. If the Congress and the Senate would get serious about cutting the legal-beagle legs out from underneath these bozos, we'd be back at the pool rather than collecting sand in our boondockers.

"You got a great gal there, Bo, a beautiful home and a business that'll just keep makin' money as long as we're both around to service the till. Every one of these boys here has done his time and served his country. I don't think any of us is looking for a last firefight, but we're sure pushin' the odds. I'd give it some thought once we've wrapped this baby up in swaddling clothes. Linda deserves more than just a sizable bank account in case you purchase the old ranchero."

Before Thornton could answer, both men heard Silver's hoarse whisper. "I got Phong, Bo! He's sittin' in my scope like a bump on a log! Scoot your ass over here and take a look. The general's got hisself a big ole rifle and a primo position from which to shoot. Must have the same idea about Canales as you do!"

Bo slithered over to where Silver lay, stretching out behind the M60 so he could peer through the scope at what Jason had found. Nodding in satisfaction once he had Phong's head in focus, the former Green Beret motioned for Hartung to pass the Win-Mag across to him. That done, all three men hurriedly rebuilt Bo's shooting platform, moving Silver's M60 slightly to the left so Jason could still cover a good portion of the plateau's lip as well as most of the steep trail Canales would have to climb. The sandbags repositioned, Thornton slid the rifle's forestock into place, then settled himself behind the huge weapon's butt.

"See what he's got with him?" asked Silver.

"Roger that. Long gun of some sort, maybe a 7.62 or even a 30.06. Scoped, fancy stock. Hunting rifle more than likely. Looks like the general's decided to drop the hammer on Canales himself in a very personal manner."

Rowe spoke up from behind the two men. "I got movement at the base of the trail! Riders, maybe five or so. All armed and moving quickly."

Frank grunted. "A little early but not so as to account for much. Gotta be a point element, which means Phong'll have to let them gain the high ground before the main body starts the climb. Al, you better alert the Apaches."

With a thumbs-up, Rowe dialed in their air support, advising the pilots of what was taking place and asking them to inform the SLAM team so he wouldn't have to spend unnecessary time on the air. Receiving an "out" from the anxious gunship commander, Rowe informed Bo they were ready to initiate on his command.

"Good!" acknowledged Thornton. "Frank? How about spotting for me. I need your glasses on Phong while I dial in Canales. When it looks like he's going do the Mexican, let me know."

"No sweat," replied the sergeant major. Frank positioned the Steiners so he was looking down at Phong's camouflaged hide, noting that the man was using a spotter also. "The general's got a sidekick, Bo. You gonna want to waste him before engaging the primary?"

Thornton had moved so he was now looking down the canyon's trail at a slight angle. The .300 was locked into his shoulder, his left hand slowly focusing the gun's impressive scope on the first of the outriders, now halfway up the cutback's grade. Hearing Frank's query, Thornton nodded, intent on identifying Canales before Phong could do so. He'd have to take the general's spotter immediately upon shifting his fire, thereby blinding the opposing sniper, whose scope would be pointing directly into the sun if he should shift the rifle's muzzle up toward Bo's position. It was the spotter who actually evaluated the shooter's targets, finding them for the rifleman and describing their location as the sniper adjusted himself to his guide's directions. This held especially true when an interdiction team was faced with multiple or surprise targets of opportunity, which Thornton would become once Phong watched the object of his wrath snatched away from him in the blink of an eye.

For the next ten minutes, each group lay as if in suspended animation while the horse-mounted recon element gingerly made its way to the level plane of the desolate plateau. The Vietnamese held their fire, their positions expertly camouflaged so that the Mexicans trotted past them without a second glance. Satisfied with what he'd found, the group's leader lifted a walkie-talkie to his mouth and spoke for several seconds. Finished, he lifted a hand and began working his way back to the craggy summit's lip, where he'd been ordered to put in security for the remainder of the caravan, just now reaching the base of the trail.

"Remember," said Thornton as he began scanning the riders below him, "I'll open the ball game with a shot on Canales. We let the Viets do the majority of the damage on the caravan, then call in the sky boys. Frank'll put me on Phong as soon as the first round goes down-range. Once that's over with it'll be Alan's job to direct the Apaches in on the Viet positions until there's no effective ground fire coming from them. In the meantime anyone you see is a target of opportunity. We got some heavy firepower with us—let's use it to good advantage.''

Another five minutes passed before Bo saw what he'd been searching for. The rider stood out from those around him for two reasons. The first was the horse, which was an impressive animal in both size and color. Secondly, Canales had dressed for the occasion, wearing a wide-brimmed Stetson and matching trail coat. Thornton ignored the four hard men surrounding the drug kingpin; they'd be dead within minutes once the Viets began blasting the hapless riders from their entrenched positions.

"Stand by!" ordered Bo. "Frank? What's Phong doing?"

Hartung, who'd been locked onto the general's position ever since he'd been ordered to spot for Bo, began describing Phong's actions. "He's excited. I can see him working the bolt and he's laying into the stock now. His spotter's jabbering a mile a minute, probably describing Canales. I'd say we're down to the last ten seconds or so, better do it or lose it, Bo."

Thornton gently laid his cheek against the smooth fiberglass stock. He'd turned the scope up to its greatest magnification, centering the cross hairs at the base of the Mexican's throat. Adjusting for the drop of the round as well as for the constant bobbing of the target in his saddle, Bo exhaled a long draft of air. Breathing easily, he snugged the stock into his shoulder, wrapping his left hand around the weapon's rear sling swivel. His forefinger resting lightly on the trigger's face, Thornton drilled

Canales with a scornful grimace through the scope's viewer. "Okay, you son of a bitch," he whispered loud enough for Frank to overhear. "Here's a little something for twelve good men you and I never knew. Payback's a motherhumper, pal!"

Bo never felt the rifle explode against his shoulder as the massive projectile roared down the custom-fluted tube and across the canyon like an express train. Even as he watched the Mexican's head evaporate in a fountain of fragmented bone and emulsified tissue, his right hand was working the gun's bolt, ejecting the spent casing and slamming a fresh round into the rifle's hungry breech. As one, the Viet ambush force opened up on the surprised smugglers, the security team blown out of its saddles as a single machine gunner ripped a hundred-round burst across their huddled mass at near point-blank range. Thornton was sliding the Win-Mag across its sandbagged base when a round from Phong's rifle chipped a huge hunk of shale away from the pile Hartung was lying behind. "He's on us!" yelled the sergeant major, his own assault rifle poking out from between a crack in the sandstone barrier.

Bo rapidly adjusted his scope so the twin heads of his next targets swam into view as if they were just fifty meters away instead of three hundred. Diem, who was spotting for Phong, raised himself a tad too high from behind his otherwise excellent cover, a pair of field glasses held tightly in one hand as he searched for the source of the hidden rifleman who'd just ruined the general's day. Phong had automatically turned his barrel on the most obvious source of the unexpected gunfire, rapping off a quick round just to buy some time as he and Diem sought to readjust their position. The Viet had watched Canales die, which had been pleasing even if it hadn't been by Phong's own hand. His men were destroying the caravan, sending riderless horses plunging back down the narrow trail, which was littered with the corpses of dead mules and wasted gunmen.

Thornton zeroed Diem within two adrenaline-fueled heartbeats. Squeezing the trigger once, he grunted as the SABOT round caught the Vietnamese square in the face, blowing the field glasses apart and sending shards of slippery skull fragments directly into the face of General Phong. A second round from the general's gun careened off the rocks below as Phong was forced to involuntarily fire. Bo worked his weapon's bolt once more, capturing the general's blood-drenched features in his scope, the cross hairs splitting the man's face into four equal quadrants. A gentle tug against the trigger sent yet one more .300-caliber missile downrange, Phong's entire body jerked upright as the bullet blew out the man's left eye socket in a flood of runny liquid and shredded brain matter. "Eye of the Tiger!" whooped Bo as Frank slapped the master shooter hard on the back. "Say good night, General 'Fuck Me–Fuck You' Phong!"

Rowe was already yelling into his hand-held mike, the Apaches airborne and visible as they swept across the plateau's arid plains at less than fifty feet above the desert. Within seconds both gun platforms were laying down long streams of machine cannon fire, rockets whooshing out of their tubes and impacting along the Viets' front as Alan directed the pilots in on targets he'd preplotted during their wait. Satisfied the gun crews were well on their own, Rowe lifted the M21 to his shoulder and began selecting targets among the Mexican smugglers still alive on the trail. With cool determination he pegged man after man, sometimes double-tapping his rifle's victims, sometimes using only one shot to deliver

Death's message. Across from him Jason Silver was eating up belt after belt of 7.62 spine busters, concentrating on the Vietnamese who were beginning to break out of their spider holes under the fury of the Apaches' guns and rockets. Frank emptied a magazine from his own weapon, changing it quickly and joining Rowe, who had nearly succeeded in clearing the trail of anything living. In the meantime Thornton confirmed Canales's death by sending his fourth round into the inert body's mass, its impact jerking the dead Mexican rearward a full foot. Working the bolt one last time, Bo selected a running figure that was nearly at the base of the trail. It would be a seven hundred-meter shot, downhill, and at a running target, with cordite smoke beginning to choke the shooter as he drew a bead on the rapidly moving man. Putting his brain on automatic pilot, Thornton relaxed for just a moment, then pulled the trigger. Far below him the object of his rifle's wrath stumbled as the bullet caught him high in the back, then fell. Bo's view of the downed man was lost as a rocket from one of the Apaches slammed into the ground near where the body lay, obscuring it in a flash of fiery heat and high-velocity fragmentation.

Bailey's concentration was on the batch of Vietnamese nearest to their position, and within minutes he'd cleared three sand-and-rock bunkers of their occupants. Shifting his fire upward, the busy narc blasted away at scurrying figures that drifted in and out of sight, pulling off when he saw the Apaches coming in low for their final strafing runs. "Cease-fire! Cease-fire!" yelled Rowe as the gunships pulled off, blasting over the top of the team's position in a roar of twin turbines and hot lead. "The SLAM team's en route and will infil just below the first Viet positions. Let's watch the fucking trail in case some of the dopers are still functional enough to shoot straight!''

Calvin nodded, keeping the snout of his 60 in line with the Viets as Silver turned his on the trail. Rowe began scanning the broad field of fire with his 21's scope, popping a round off here and there as targets presented themselves. Frank was gabbing with the chopper pilots as they began to hover above the ravished desert's floor, spilling their loads in rapid succession as the SLAM commandos quickly took the field. Above it all Bo Thornton gently lay his rifle down, searching for a cigar in his breast pocket and then lighting it with a wooden match from his survival kit. The mixed sounds of combat failed to distract him from the pleasure he was feeling at nailing both the Mexican and General Phong within heartbeats of each other. Now a good man and his team could rest easy, now a bunch of hard-working Vietnamese could get on with their lives without living in fear and mistrust. More importantly, a huge amount of dope would never hit the streets of America. If just one kid could walk away without the stain of drug abuse clouding his life, then the entire effort was worth it as far as Thornton was concerned. Lying back and watching his men at work, the weary commando leader puffed slowly at his cigar, a wide smile on his face as he began to relax for the first time in days.

"You got another one of them there stogies?" asked Frank, the last of his magazines emptied in a three-round burst at a possibly still-alive dope smuggler.

"Abso-fucking-lutely," replied Thornton, digging a long brown tube out from his pocket. "You want me to smoke it for you, too?"

"Nawww," laughed Frank as he drew a chestful of the fragrant smoke deeply into his lungs, "you already got one of your own . . . asshole!"

Above them the choppers peeled off and headed for an LZ hastily being marked by two SLAM-dunk artists with smoke grenades. The sound of gunfire was lessening now, only single shots echoing down the canyon as teams of agents searched for the living with the sole intention of making them dead. "Let's get the fuck outta here," offered Bo as his team quit firing. "I've had enough of this bullshit for one day. The federal boys can finish the job without us. Alan? Get one of the hawks up on the extraction frequency and let's go home!"

"You got it, boss!" exclaimed a beaming Alan Rowe, the radio's handset snugged up under his bearding chin.

"Airborne and Amen!" added Frank.

As one, they waited until the steady drone of an empty Blackhawk became a roar, its open doors promising sanctuary from the hell they'd just experienced, from the hell they'd just delivered.

SPRINGBLADE was going home.

# CHAPTER

## 21

Bo lay in their bed, his body lightly frosted with sweat from their lovemaking. He had only a sheet pulled over him as the bed's covers lay unceremoniously on the floor, where they'd been shoved sometime during the evening. Downstairs he heard Linda padding around in the kitchen, the sound of the coffee pot beginning to perk.

Thornton rolled over so he could stare out at the sea. It was gray outside, a strong coastal wind blowing hard across the ocean's choppy surface. The beach far below was deserted except for the odd gull that swooped low, looking for a scrambling sand crab or a piece of ravished fish. Inside the house it was warm, the remnants of last night's fire still glowing brightly in the massive stove they'd installed in the bedroom. The former soldier smiled at how far he'd come from the bad old days of living in a barracks on post. If they could see me now, he thought.

The team had disbanded twenty-four hours after returning to the DEA mission support site. Billings had been there to meet them, Bailey conducting much of the after-action briefing, with a team of agents collecting every bit of information they could from Rowe, Hartung, and Silver. Bo never saw the SLAM team again, hearing they'd cleaned up what they could find, blowing half the canyon over the remains of those slaughtered between its walls. The dope had been stacked into a huge pile, then rocketed by one of the Apaches after it had refueled and rearmed. Overall, the mission was considered a success, with Phong's disappearance announced in the news media as unlawful flight to avoid prosecution. Canales's death was ignored; after all, he was not a U.S. citizen, so who gave a fat rat's ass? They'd been paid in full and given first class tickets home. There wasn't much left to say other than "see you next time."

The quiet chirp of Bo's portable phone broke his train of thought. Lifting the instrument, he punched in on the line, waiting a moment as if deciding whether to take the call or not. Choosing to live dangerously, he answered. As he was listening to the caller, Linda sauntered into their room, a tray full of food and drink in her hands. Bo glanced quickly at her, indicating with a sweep of his hand that she should sit next to him on the mussed bed. Doing so, the girl handed the naked warrior a steaming mug of coffee, watching him as he only nodded and grunted into the phone's mouthpiece.

"Bailey wanted you to know ASAP, Mr. Thornton. Sorry about the news. We're doing all we can, but Calvin feels you and your gang might want a hand in what's cooking over at Billings's office. I'll call you back sometime this evening. You let me know what you want to do, if anything. Okay?"

Thornton rubbed his free hand across his brow. The coffee was excellent, Linda's soft hand resting lightly on his thigh as she drank her own. "Roger that. I need to make some calls first. Keep me informed and thanks for the thought. Out here."

Linda watched Bo's face as he stared impassively at the wall. Something was up, something that didn't please the man she'd decided she'd be staying with come hell or high water. While he'd been gone Linda had done some serious soul searching. He was as real a man as the girl had ever met, and she realized he would never hurt her intentionally, because he loved her as much as she did him. Their conversation while he'd been away had haunted her. Who was she to demand he quit doing something he believed in? If she couldn't handle it, then it was she who needed to adapt, adjust, or abdicate what hold he allowed her to have over him. He'd earned the right to be Beaumont "Bo" Thornton, and she could either take him or leave him as he was. "Bad news?" she ventured, rubbing his neck gently.

"Mike Bannion is missing in Burma. His chopper went down several days ago after a raid on a drug storage site. American rangers went in and combed the area. They found no survivors, but no Mike either. Two days ago a second search team discovered a note several hundred meters from the crash site. It was from Mike. He said he was okay, but being chased. Billings wants to get him out if at all possible."

Linda sat, immobile, Bo's words hitting her like a cold shower. Mike Bannion was one of her favorite people. He was the high school hero in many ways. Big, blond, and as gentle as he was tough, Mike had treated her like royalty when they'd met. "Burma's so far from here," was all she could say.

"He's one of ours. I'm gonna call Frank, Jason, the whole crew. Calvin thinks Conrad may ask us to go in after him. You know I have to; we owe him for saving our asses in San Francisco. If it pisses you off . . ."

"Beaumont Thornton!" the girl exclaimed, standing so abruptly she spilled her coffee on the thick carpet, where she now stood with both hands firmly planted on her shapely hips. "Don't you *ever* insinuate I wouldn't back you up when it comes to Mike or any one of the guys! If Conrad what's-his-name will let me, I'll go too, if there's any way I can help the team. I'm no bleeding liberal wimp, mister! Remember, we've been through five of these things together, and you haven't seen me pack my bags yet. You just finish your coffee and get cleaned up. It's too early to get everyone on the phone at once, but we can com-link at 1100 hours *no problema*. If Mike's in trouble, we gotta help, end of discussion!"

Thornton stared, slack-jawed, at the angry girl. Shit-fire, he thought to himself. What have I got here? Grabbing her around the waist, he eased her back into bed, nuzzling her as she bit playfully at his shoulders and throat. "You sound mean enough to take with us, little lady. Watch yourself or I might book you a slot."

Linda stopped her nibbling, gazing softly into Bo's eyes as she spoke. "You do that, buster. Five times I've sat back here and waited for you to walk through that door. Five lousy, lonely times. I can shoot, move, and communicate. You'll need everyone you can get if Mike's still alive. Take me, please!"

So he did.

# HIGH-TECH ADVENTURES BY BESTSELLING AUTHORS

____**DAY OF THE CHEETAH**

**Dale Brown** 0-425-12043-0/$5.50

In Dale Brown's newest *New York Times* bestseller, Lieutenant Colonel Patrick McClanahan's plane, the Cheetah, must begin the greatest high-tech chase of all time.

____**AMBUSH AT OSIRAK**

**Herbert Crowder** 0-515-09932-5/$4.50

Israel is poised to attack the Iraqi nuclear production plant at Osirak. But the Soviets have supplied Iraq with the ultimate super-weapon . . . and the means to wage nuclear war.

____**ROLLING THUNDER**

**Mark Berent** 0-515-10190-7/$4.95

The best of the Air Force face the challenge of Vietnam in "a taut, exciting tale . . . Berent is the real thing!"—Tom Clancy

____**FLIGHT OF THE OLD DOG**

**Dale Brown** 0-425-10893-7/$4.95

The unthinkable has happened: The Soviets have mastered Star Wars technology. And when its killer laser is directed across the globe, America's only hope is a battle-scarred bomber—the Old Dog Zero One.

---

For Visa, MasterCard and American Express orders call: 1-800-631-8571

FOR MAIL ORDERS: CHECK BOOK(S). FILL OUT COUPON. SEND TO:

**BERKLEY PUBLISHING GROUP**
390 Murray Hill Pkwy., Dept. B
East Rutherford, NJ 07073

NAME _____

ADDRESS_____

CITY_____

STATE_____ ZIP _____

PLEASE ALLOW 6 WEEKS FOR DELIVERY.
PRICES ARE SUBJECT TO CHANGE

POSTAGE AND HANDLING:
$1.00 for one book, 25¢ for each additional. Do not exceed $3.50.

BOOK TOTAL                    $ ____

POSTAGE & HANDLING           $ ____

APPLICABLE SALES TAX         $ ____
(CA, NJ, NY, PA)

TOTAL AMOUNT DUE             $ ____

PAYABLE IN US FUNDS.
(No cash orders accepted.)

231a

# HIGH-TECH, HARD-EDGED ACTION!
## All-new series!

__STEELE J.D. Masters 1-55773-219-1/$3.50
Lt. Donovan Steele—one of the best cops around, until he was killed. Now he's been rebuilt--the perfect combination of man and machine, armed with the firepower of a high-tech army!

__COLD STEELE J.D. Masters 1-55773-278-7/$3.50
The hard-hitting adventures of Lt. Donovan Steele continue.

__FREEDOM'S RANGERS Keith William Andrews 0-425-11643-3/$3.95
An elite force of commandos fights the battles of the past to save America's future—this time it's 1923 and the Rangers are heading to Munich to overthrow Adolf Hitler!

__FREEDOM'S RANGERS #2: RAIDERS OF THE REVOLUTION
Keith William Andrews 0-425-11832-0/$2.95
The Rangers travel back to the late 18th century to ensure that Washington is successful.

__TANKWAR Larry Steelbaugh 0-425-11741-3/$3.50
On the battlefields of World War III, Sergeant Max Tag and his crew take on the Soviet army with the most sophisticated high-tech tank ever built.

__SPRINGBLADE Greg Walker 1-55773-266-3/$2.95
Bo Thornton—Vietnam vet, Special Forces, Green Beret. Now retired, he's leading a techno-commando team—men who'll take on the dirtiest fighting jobs and won't leave until justice is done.

__THE MARAUDERS Michael McGann 0-515-10150-8/$2.95
World War III is over, but enemy forces are massing in Europe, plotting the ultimate takeover. And the Marauders—guerrilla freedom fighters—aren't waiting around for the attack. They're going over to face it head-on!

---

**Check book(s). Fill out coupon. Send to:**

**BERKLEY PUBLISHING GROUP**
390 Murray Hill Pkwy., Dept. B
East Rutherford, NJ 07073

NAME_____

ADDRESS_____

CITY_____

STATE_____ZIP_____

**PLEASE ALLOW 6 WEEKS FOR DELIVERY.
PRICES ARE SUBJECT TO CHANGE
WITHOUT NOTICE.**

**POSTAGE AND HANDLING:**
$1.00 for one book, 25¢ for each additional. Do not exceed $3.50.

BOOK TOTAL                      $_____

POSTAGE & HANDLING              $_____

APPLICABLE SALES TAX            $_____
(CA, NJ, NY, PA)

TOTAL AMOUNT DUE                $_____

**PAYABLE IN US FUNDS.**
(No cash orders accepted.)

243a